MW00366800

Return to the Chapel of Eternal Love

Marriage Stories from Las Vegas

By Stephen Murray

Congratulations !

Steph Murray

Return to the Chapel of Eternal Love

Marriage Stories from Las Vegas

Copyright ©2015, Stephen Murray

ISBN: 978-0-9911940-1-8
$14.95us

Cover by: Cynthia Carbajal

This is a work of fiction. Names, characters, businesses, places, events and incidents are either the products of the author's imagination or used in a fictitious manner. Any resemblance to actual persons, living or dead, or actual places and events is purely coincidental.

All rights reserved. No part of this publication may be translated, reproduced, or transmitted in any form or by any means, electronic or mechanical, including photocopying and recording, or by any information storage and retrieval system, without the written permission of the copyright owner.

Acknowledgments

To my family and friends—RJ, Sue, Grayham, Louise, Maria and Kolleen for all their support and encouragement.

To my writers group—Sue, Gail, Deborah, Nancy and Donelle for all their invaluable advice and suggestions throughout the process.

To Brian Rouff and staff, Imagine Communications of Henderson, Nevada.

To James Kelly, Aspects of Writing.

To s h 'Sue' Montgomery for all her help with editing and for making the process a joy.

Chapter 1

Winds of Change

Pastor Glen opened his mailbox and was elated to see Rosemary's return address on one of the envelopes. It had been almost five years since he had made the trip back to the Chapel of Eternal Love—the shrine he built in Las Vegas as a tribute to his wife, Laura. He held fond memories of Rosemary, manager of the chapel, and had not forgotten her kindness to him or the dinner she had rustled up in her warm and inviting home that evening. It had been many years since he'd savored a home cooked meal prepared so lovingly. He recalled listening to her stories of the couples and their ceremonies during the many years she spent as wedding coordinator. Their frequent correspondence since was one of the few regular events in his life he relished and eagerly looked forward to.

His mind was still alert for being eighty years old. Walking every day kept him agile. Through the bitter Wyoming winters, as it was now, he always donned a scarf knitted by one of his former parishioners and sported a thick winter coat as he walked through the neighboring woods, his cane being his support. He loved the solitude, the fresh, crisp air and the exercise.

Today, he decided to forego his daily walk in anticipation of the contents of Rosemary's letter. As he exhaled, he saw his breath turn to fog in the cold air. Slowly, Pastor Glen made his way back along the paved path to his small, rustic cottage that had been his home for over fifty years. Well-worn rugs were scattered across the wooden floor of the sparsely furnished living room. A mantle shelf over the fireplace displayed many discolored and faded photos of his Laura. An old-fashioned mahogany desk dominated one corner of the room. An unevenly stacked and disheveled mass of papers covered the top of his desk and were stuck in the many little carved nooks and crannies meant for storing paper clips and postage stamps. A small, light-brown sofa covered with assorted cushions sat against one wall. Occupying the center of the room was his favorite comfortable armchair facing the fireplace, with its back to the untidy desk.

Upon entering the front door, Pastor Glen removed his shoes and put on his relatively new and comfortable, dark-blue slippers which were a birthday gift from one of his kind neighbors. He placed his mail on the small table alongside his armchair and headed toward the kitchen, rubbing his cold hands to keep them warm. It was lunchtime, and a pot of chicken noodle soup was warming on his stove. He switched off the gas, poured the steaming broth into a large mug which he took with him to the living room, ensconced himself in the armchair and wrapped a heavy blanket over his legs. He tried not to light the fire, unless it was icy cold. The logs he had to carry from the shed were heavy and tired him. He took a sip of his lunch, placed the mug on the table, and opened the letter from Rosemary. He noticed the date of December 10th at the top.

"*Dear Pastor Glen,*" he read in her now familiar scrawl.

"It is with a heavy heart that I write this letter to you. Very soon I will be celebrating my sixtieth birthday. I will also have worked at The Chapel of Eternal Love for just over twenty-five years. But sadly, it is now time for me to take early retirement.

My older sister, Katie, and her husband are moving to Florida. Katie has been keeping her eye on our spry eighty-five-year-old mother, who has lived in the same house since she was married and refuses to move. It is my turn to pick up the baton from where my sister will leave off. My mother lives just outside of Carson City, which as you know, is in the Northern part of Nevada. Buster and I will go there to be with her.

Buster, unfortunately, is getting frail. He is now almost nine years old. As I think I mentioned to you before, he finds it difficult to make it up and down the steps into the office at the chapel. Father Mark was kind enough to build a small cement ramp next to the steps, making it easier for Buster to go in and out. Even so, it is still hard for him. His stubby little legs don't quite have the stamina they used to. Surprisingly, his knack for sniffing out the "good guys" who come to the chapel and providing his cautionary growls to the unsavory characters, remains. Fortunately, there aren't too many of those.

As you know, the chapel has been my life and love. I just dread the thought of having to leave. I will treasure the cherished memories always. But as a minister you are also aware, duty must always come first. I have tendered my resignation to Father Mark, giving him six weeks notice. My last day will be January 19th.

Las Vegas is getting geared up for the Christmas season and everything looks so festive. We are already deluged with Christmas cards from across the world from people who married at the chapel. Some I remember, some, unfortunately, I don't. But it is nice they remember their special day and our part in making it so. What an incredible legacy you have left, Pastor Glen.

As we count our blessings, I wish you good health and much joy at this festive time. Do hope you are surviving your winter and look forward to hearing from you soon.

Fondly, Rosemary.

Pastor Glen was devastated. He had come to acknowledge how much of Laura's legacy was due to Rosemary's caring and compassionate nature. Her devotion to the chapel was absolute. However, he recognized she needed to be there for her family. The philosophy of honoring one's father and mother was one he'd espoused in his many sermons to parishioners over the years.

Mindful of the fact that Monday was Rosemary's day off from work, he seized the opportunity to call Father Mark Roades at the chapel. After rummaging around his desk, he located his address book and dialed the number he had listed. He hoped a fitting farewell party had been planned for his friend.

Almost immediately, the phone was answered.

"The Chapel of Eternal Love, Father Roades at your service."

"Good afternoon, Father Roades. My name is Pastor Glen Phillips, and I'm calling from Wyoming. You don't know me …" He was cut short.

"But indeed, I do, Pastor Glen. Everyone associated with the Chapel of Eternal Love is aware of its history and your role in it. It is an honor to speak with you, sir." Father Roades, a balding man in his late forties, whose round, jovial face seemed to always sport a perpetual smile was pleasantly surprised by the unexpected call.

"You are too kind," Pastor Glen responded.

The two men of faith engaged in discussion on matters regarding the state of religion for a short while before Pastor Glen raised the subject of Rosemary's departure.

"Father Roades, you are probably wondering what prompted my call today. You may or may not know, but five years ago, I stopped by the chapel on my way to a retreat in California. It was before you started there. I spent some time with Rosemary and was in awe of her devotion in keeping my memory of Laura alive. The chapel really does appear to be the love of her life. Today, I received the disturbing news that she is leaving the chapel after twenty five years to take care of her elderly mother," said Pastor Glen.

"Yes," Mark Roades responded. "I feel sad that she is leaving. I've yet to find a suitable replacement, or indeed, any replacement at all, for that matter. It is very troubling. I've been praying every day. As you must know, we're not in a position to pay a lot of money, so the individual I hire must work from the heart and for all the right reasons."

"Well, Rosemary is definitely irreplaceable," replied Pastor Glen. "No one will ever quite take her place. But the reason for my call is to ask if there are any plans for a farewell celebration for her."

Father Mark felt embarrassed. "I must confess I've been remiss in giving that any thought. I do know on the Saturday evening, after her final day, some friends are having a small dinner party for her, to which I've been invited. Truth is, I've been so involved in trying to find a replacement, I've not even considered a farewell party … but that's no excuse."

"Well," said Pastor Glen, "I doubt Rosemary is aware of the significance of her retirement date, but it happens to be the fifth anniversary of my visit to the chapel. I was thinking of maybe doing something bold for her departure. I don't know if it would be possible, or not, to have the couples who were married on that day to return to help give Rosemary a fitting farewell party. The night we met, she gave me quite a detailed description of the couples who were married earlier that day. There is no doubt in my mind she had an impact on many of them. Do you still have the documents with the contact information?"

"What a splendid idea. I wish I had thought of doing this. I'm sure we could make it happen—and you're right. It would be memorable."

"Well, I would certainly be happy to write the letters if you have the information," offered Pastor Glen.

Mark Roades considered the age of the chapel's founder and what a laborious effort it would be for him. "I appreciate the gesture," he responded. "But time is pretty much of the essence. Fortunately, contact information with phones numbers are requested on the forms. Rosemary keeps copious and meticulous records of all the documents for seven years. I don't know why, she just does. I should be able to track the information with relative ease." Not wishing to cut the pastor out of the planning altogether, he continued, "I'll make a list of the numbers, and maybe you can call some of the couples. Give me your phone number, let me think about what type of party we could have, figure out a budget, and I'll get back to you."

"Well, I don't have a huge amount of money," said Pastor Glen, "but I would be more than happy to give a portion of my savings for the event. I don't drive anymore due to my age, so I doubt I would be able to attend. But I'd really like Rosemary to leave knowing how much she was appreciated."

Father Mark knew this was not a light hearted gesture Pastor Glen was making and was truly moved by the generosity and the high esteem in which he seemed to hold Rosemary. *I will have to find a way for him to attend*, he thought. "Hopefully, that won't be necessary," he said somberly. "But I will get back to you very shortly." He wrote down the Wyoming phone number, and the two gentlemen hung up.

Pastor Glen lay back in his chair, folded his arms, and gave up a silent prayer. He felt good about his newly found friend's commitment.

Father Mark immediately went to the cabinet with the prior years files. As expected, all were labeled and easily identifiable. *How true-to-form Rosemary is*, he marveled, opening the cabinet with the appropriate year's records. He flicked through the months locating the day in question and quickly wrote down the names and the cell numbers of each of the participants. As he transcribed the information, he noticed two couples listed with no phone numbers or addresses. *How odd*, he thought. He also observed Rosemary's notes on those who never actually married, but decided if they could be located he would invite them, too. Immediately, recognizing a name, he decided it was as good a place as any to start. He picked up the phone and dialed the number.

Chapter 2
The Gamble Paid Off

Father Roades waited patiently for an answer as he listened to the familiar ringing sound at the other end of the telephone line.

"Hello," said the soft, dulcet tone of a female's voice when the phone was eventually answered.

"May I speak to Prudence Latimer?" he enquired.

"This is she, but the name is now Prudence Nelson."

Pru was sitting in her office on the top floor of her new luxury hotel, Bella Del Mundo, in Las Vegas. It was an office shared with her husband, Chad. No expense had been spared with the furnishings. The sapphire-blue sofas, matching velvet drapes, and Wedgewood colored carpet displayed a quiet, understated elegance. It reflected Pru's calm demeanor and gentile personality.

Mark Roades looked at Rosemary's completed wedding forms and realized he probably should have asked for Pru's new husband. As everyone did in Las Vegas, he was aware of Pru Latimer's status. The Latimers and their premiere hotel chains were known throughout the world. He remembered all the publicity when her first husband passed away and the speculation as to whether she would be able to run the conglomerate alone.

"Of course. Forgive me, Mrs. Nelson. My name is Mark Roades, and I'm the minister at the Chapel of Eternal Love here in Las Vegas."

"Ah, yes. I know it. I was married there myself a few years ago. But I don't recall it being a Father Roades who married my husband and me."

He chuckled. "No, it wasn't. I've only been here three years."

Pru swiveled slowly in her chair and turned to look at the breathtaking view in front of her, wondering what was prompting the call. "What can I do for you, Father?"

"Well, I don't know if you remember our manager and wedding coordinator, Rosemary ... " He paused to see if there was a sign of recognition.

Pru laughed. "Of course I do. We were old school friends. We'd lost touch, but when I remarried, we picked up where we left off. We have lunch together on her day off every couple of months or so. We're due to meet again shortly. How is she doing? Nothing's wrong with her is there?" She suddenly became serious as she contemplated that her friend might be ill.

"She's just fine, Mrs. Nelson. But I'm sure you know her mother is unwell, and Rosemary will be leaving soon. Her last day is the day of your fifth wedding anniversary. I'm trying to bring together all the couples who married that day for a farewell party."

"What a truly lovely idea. How very thoughtful of you to consider such a thing."

Mark was embarrassed. "Well, I wish I could take credit. Actually, it was Pastor Glen, the founder of the chapel who thought of it. Apparently, he and Rosemary communicate by mail. She informed him of her plans, and he called to see if he could help contribute to her farewell party. I had to confess I hadn't thought about one."

"Ah yes, dear Pastor Glen. Rosemary has spoken often of him. Well, where is the party to be held?"

"I haven't figured anything out, yet. I only heard from Pastor Glen today. You're the first call I've made. Of course, I recognized your name on the list of those who married that day. Right now, I'm just making preliminary calls to see who I can establish contact with. I'll follow up with details later."

The door to the office opened, and Pru turned around in her chair. Chad entered the room and headed toward her desk to give her a kiss. *He's as handsome now as he was the day we first met,* she thought. She recalled all her doubts on her wedding day, as she knew the marriage would be a gamble. He came around behind her and kissed her softly on the cheek, gently massaging her shoulders.

"Father Roades, my husband has just come into the room. Let me put you on the speaker phone."

"Who is it?" Chad asked.

"Honey, this is the new minister who works at the Chapel of Eternal Love. Because Rosemary is retiring he's organizing a goodbye party for her and is inviting all the people who were married five years ago on the date she's leaving."

"How do we fit in? Do you want to reserve a private function room at one of our hotels, sir?"

The minister thought the voice of Pru's husband sounded much younger than hers. He looked down at the ages listed on his marriage forms and observed there was a significant age difference between the two. Of course, it was not his position to cast judgment.

"No, honey," Pru said abruptly. "The day Rosemary retires is the day of our fifth anniversary. We're invited guests. The minister is just in the early planning stage. We're his first call. He doesn't even know where it will be held, yet."

"Why can't we have it here?" Chad asked.

Father Roades laughed quietly. "I doubt if reserving a party room at *any* of your hotels will be in our budget, Mr. Nelson."

Chad continued. "Nonsense. We can spring for it right here, can't we, sweetheart? After all, Rosemary is a friend of yours."

Pru put her hand over her shoulder and patted those of her husband's. "Good idea. What and where do you have in mind?"

"Right here at the Bella Del Mundo. How many people are we talking about? Thirty? Forty?"

"Somewhere around that number. Depends on how many people I can get in touch with. After five years, it might be hard to locate some of the people," Mark replied.

"That's not a problem. We have a private eye on retainer. Any couples you have trouble contacting, just give us a call. We'll put him to work."

"I'm truly overwhelmed by your generosity. A party at your hotel will be infinitely better than anything I could put together."

"It's a win-win," said Chad. It will be good for Bella Del Mundo. After Christmas and New Year's, it will be quiet, and it's before Super Bowl. Presumably, some of the people will be from out of state so when they return home, they'll tell all their friends about their stay with us. It will be excellent publicity. I was thinking of reserving the Celebration Room, sweetheart. What do you think?"

Pru marveled at how her husband had such a firm grasp on all the aspects of her hotels and had such quick solutions. "The Celebration Room will be perfect, if it's not already reserved."

"Just leave the details to me. I'll check the availability, and if it's not, I'll find something suitable. And we'll have invitations made up. Just provide us with the addresses, sir. I'll hold a block of rooms immediately."

"Your party is in good hands, Father Roades," Pru responded warmly and proudly. "Is there anything else?"

"Well, since you mentioned about helping locate some of the people, there *are* a couple of names on my list where the telephone numbers are missing, and there are no addresses, either. Rosemary is so efficient I can't believe there's no information. One name is Rosa De La Corazon."

"That problem is easily solved. Rosa De La Corazon works right here in our hotel." Pru was pleased she could locate one of the people. "Her story is a long and complicated one, but don't worry about her. She'll be at Rosemary's party. I can guarantee that. Who else?"

"There's a Cory Moran and a Samantha Jameson. I have no other details."

"I'll put our private eye right on it," said Chad. He moved around the desk and scribbled the names on a notepad. "Don't worry. We'll track them down. I'll get working on this, Father. Do we have your phone number so I can keep in touch as things develop?"

Father Roades gave his contact number and said, "May God bless you both. I'm so grateful. It will be very special for Rosemary. By the way, I would like it to be a surprise."

"Consider it a reverse confession, Father. Your secret is safe with us."

Pru turned and glared at her husband. There was still the odd occasion when he could be so tactless.

They hung up the phone, and Chad smiled and gazed into Pru's still piercingly soft, blue eyes. "Since this is the time for confessions, do you have time for one?" he asked.

"Absolutely," she replied. "But only if you have time for one afterwards."

"Since we're talking about private eyes, do you still have one follow me from time to time to see whether I am gambling and chasing women?"

She looked at him seriously, directing her eyes into his. "Good heavens. How did you know about that? That was ages ago, long before we married. But in answer to your question, no."

Chad smiled and winked at her. "Your turn."

She lit a cigarette and inhaled. "Was my faith in you justified or misplaced?"

He grinned again but then looked solemn. "I've never gambled from the day we met ... nor, have I been with another woman. I love you so much, Pru. I've not forgotten our wedding day when I overheard you saying to Rosemary that our marriage was a gamble."

"It was," replied Pru. "But it's paid off."

Chad picked up the music box, with the dancing ballerina, from the top of Pru's desk. He'd given it to her when they first met, and he liked that she was sentimental and kept it where she could see it as she worked. He realized it was one of her treasured possessions.

"I'll go see what I can do regarding this party," he said as he wound the key on the bottom of the box. The ballerina now twirling, he placed it back on the desk and turned to leave, blowing her a kiss.

As she watched him leave the office, Pru listened to the sound of Chopin's "Nocturne" now emanating from the music box and thought back over the last five joyous years they had shared together.

Her tender heart melted.

Chapter 3

Memories

Mark was pleased with his first call. How fortuitous so many of the issues were already resolved for Rosemary's party through his discussion with Pru and Chad. *Indeed, perhaps God does work in mysterious ways,* he thought, even though he knew it was a biblical misquote.

He looked through the papers of those who married that day and, not wishing to disturb people during their dinner time, decided to call the local numbers since he was unsure of the times zones of the long distance ones. *I'll call the out of state numbers tomorrow.*

He dialed a local number. A very soft, frail sounding voice said, "Hello," at the other end of the line. Mark quickly looked at the couple's ages listed on the license form and saw seventy-five listed for both. *My goodness, this couple is eighty years old. Bless their hearts.* He introduced himself and explained the reason for his call.

"How very kind of you, Father Roades," Sarah Windmeyer responded slowly. "But I don't think Oscar and I will be able to attend."

"I'm sorry to hear that," he replied. "I'm sure Rosemary will remember you and your husband and will miss you."

"Well, I certainly remember her. She was a sweet lady and was very kind to us. Does she still have that little dog?"

"Buster? Oh, absolutely. He'll be moving with her up north."

"That's nice. Yes, well I'll be moving, too." She spoke slowly and deliberately continuing the pleasantries.

"Oh? Are you and your husband moving to be close to family?" he said, conveying genuine interest.

"No." She paused, fighting back the tears she felt welling up in her eyes. "This house is far too big for me to live in alone." Father Roades heard her voice catch as if she was about to cry. He sensed a sadness as she continued, "My husband is now in a memory care facility." She started to sob. He remained quiet. After a short while she collected herself. "I do not drive at all, and when I visit Oscar the bus trips are exhausting for me. Besides, the emptiness of this huge home is more than I can bear. I've found a little apartment within walking distance of where my husband is."

"I am so sorry, Mrs. Windmeyer. I can only imagine how difficult things must be for you. I hope your families are being supportive."

"I wish that were the case, but sadly, no. They're helping to get things packed and will help me move, but his own children haven't visited him since he moved into the care facility six months ago. They claim it is too hard for them to deal with."

"Well, try not to be too judgmental. That could very well be the truth. Everyone has their own limitations and ways of dealing with issues."

"Perhaps. It's just not a good situation all round."

"How often do you see your husband now?"

"I try and visit Oscar every day, but I only stay for two hours. We have lunch and then we sit in the garden and hold hands. He gets very distraught when I leave. The sad thing is he calls me Emily now. That was the name of his first wife. They were married for fifty years, as was I to my first husband, Rex."

"Does it bother you that he calls you Emily?"

She thought for a minute. "No, not really. It did at first, but I know he doesn't mean to. The important thing is he recognizes my face when I visit, and he beams when he sees me walk through the front door. Of course, he talks about events, places and people who were part of his life before we met. I feel I've learned so much more about him since his mind has become confused. He sometimes focuses on periods in his life that he might not have otherwise discussed."

"It must be very difficult for you. If I may say so, Mrs. Windmeyer, you're a remarkably courageous woman."

She laughed rather quietly and nervously. "Well, I don't see myself quite like that. After Rex passed, my life was empty and meaningless. Then I met Oscar and we got married."

"Where did you actually meet?"

She laughed again, very timidly. "We met at the cemetery. My Rex and his Emily passed on the same day. We would both visit the cemetery and sit with our loved ones. We found solace there, and ultimately found comfort in each other. He brought happiness to my life and helped erase the dark, lonely days and nights. We talked about our previous spouses, naturally, and shared our memories. Oscar was very strong in many ways, and somehow very reassuring."

"You really are very brave Mrs. Windmeyer—and an inspiration."

"You're just being kind. Originally, Oscar helped with

the loneliness, and now he has given my life new meaning—a sense of purpose. I will not leave him. As long as he recognizes my face—even if he does have my name confused—I will be there for him, as long as the good Lord allows. I have had a wonderful life, and two wonderful husbands. Yet, with the holidays here, I'm just not feeling that holiday spirit. I am so blessed, yet I feel so guilty."

Mark Roades sat quietly as he listened to the wisdom, compassion, and sadness in Sarah's voice.

"Why, will you just listen to me carrying on?" Sarah suddenly sounded flustered. "I can't imagine what came over me. I've imposed on you—a perfect stranger. You're a minister at a wedding chapel and must have so much to attend to. I feel so silly. You really must forgive me."

"No apology necessary. That is part of who I am. I'm here to listen and help. And if there is any way I can assist with the move, or if ever you need someone to talk to, you know the number of the chapel. It hasn't changed. Please feel free to call me, Mrs. Windmeyer." *I should probably make it a point to call her myself on a regular basis*, he thought.

"Thank you, Father. You were too kind to listen to me."

There was a brief silence.

"I would like you to think about coming to Rosemary's party. I feel a change of scene and mixing with other people will do you the world of good. It is being held at the new hotel and casino Bella Del Mundo. There will not be a huge crowd attending, but I'm certainly hoping everyone who was married that day will try and be there for Rosemary."

"Well, as I mentioned earlier, I don't drive any more or

go out alone. In Las Vegas there are just too many drunks on the road."

"I could certainly arrange for you to be picked up from your home and returned when the party is over. I don't imagine for a minute it will be a late evening."

There was no response from the other end of the telephone line.

"Will you at least think about it?" he pleaded. "How long has it been since you went out for an evening or to a special event? I'd guess, probably not since your husband moved into memory care."

"You're right about that. I haven't been out."

"It would be good for you to have some "balance" in your life. Loyalty and dedication are commendable, but you also need to keep up your own strength."

"You're right. I *will* think about it."

"Good. What if I give you a call next week? See if you've changed your mind about the party, and make sure you're doing well."

"Thank you. I'd like that," she said. "And thank you so much for thinking of Oscar and me ... and for listening," she added sheepishly.

"Not at all. It was a pleasure speaking with you. Goodnight, Mrs. Windmeyer, and may God bless you."

They hung up. He looked at the marriage license. *There's one of God's angels right here on earth,* he thought.

Sarah reflected on the conversation with the minister. *What a very kind man. He must think I'm a complete fool for jabbering on and on.*

She looked around the living room with all the half-packed boxes. She would be glad when her own move was final. Suddenly, feeling a chill she went to the kitchen to make a cup of coffee in the microwave. *While that is heating up, I think I'll get myself something warm to put on.* She headed upstairs toward the bedroom and the huge adjacent walk-in closet. Lifting a nice warm woolen cardigan from one of the shelves, she looked at all the dresses hanging there.

What shall I wear if I do go to the party? she wondered.

She started to separate the dresses on the rack one by one, pulling out appropriate ones as she went, her coffee, heating in the microwave, totally forgotten.

Chapter 4

Happy Holidays

Giovanni looked admiringly at how his wife had set the dining room table, representing their differing backgrounds, marveling at her ability to blend the Christmas and Hanukkah observances. The white tablecloth with the streamer in traditional blue and the menorah as the centerpiece represented Becky's Hebrew heritage. As if to stress the holiday, she had randomly scattered chocolate gold coins down the center of the table. The six china plates with the Christmas tree motif and matching napkins certainly acknowledged his Christian upbringing.

"Both of our parents should be very happy," he said quietly to his wife, as she entered the room to give the table a final glance before inviting their families to sit down for the dinner she had so lavishly and lovingly prepared.

"Don't bet on it," she replied tartly, while indiscriminately rearranging a couple of the gold coins. "You know how they are."

"Maybe we shouldn't have tried to combine the holidays after all," he said.

"We didn't have much choice. You know we always have Christmas at your parents' home and spend Hanukkah with mine. When I told them we were going away skiing for Christmas, it made sense to have them here for a joint celebration. At least, our going away didn't seem to set off a family storm. They both understood—or at least they seemed to." She shrugged.

"Maybe, we should have just skipped seeing either of the folks during the holidays this year," Giovanni said with a tone of reservation.

"Too late now," Becky said nonchalantly, reaching to give her husband a kiss on the cheek. "Go ahead and bring them in and get them seated. I'll bring in the appetizer."

She disappeared into the kitchen as Giovanni headed to the living room.

"Esther and Jacob, Mama and Pop, time for dinner. Don't worry about the drinks, I'll take them in."

"It's really such a pleasure to see you both again," Esther said, rising from her chair, addressing Giovanni's parents, Gina and Mario. "I can't remember the last time."

Becky heard the comment from the kitchen and rolled her eyes, knowing the comment from her mother was a not so subtle jab. "I do," she called, as she laid the salad onto the small plates, making sure the colorful presentation was attractively arranged. "It was a week before we were married at the Chapel of Eternal Love. Remember? The wedding none of you attended. We all had dinner together."

Giovanni, not wishing the line of conversation to go further, tactfully changed the subject. He did not care for confrontations to which his wife often seemed oblivious. "Esther, you're sitting here next to me." He pulled back the chair and waited for her to be seated. "Jacob, why don't you sit there between your wife and daughter?" He pointed to the seat next to Esther. "Pop, please sit across from Jacob.

Mama, you can sit between me and Pop." As he held her chair, Gina looked confused as she observed the table. *Nothing seems coordinated here. Whoever heard of blue for Christmas?* she thought, but decided to keep her opinions to herself.

Becky emerged from the kitchen with six salad plates neatly positioned on a tray which she placed on the buffet. As she served, Giovanni brought the drinks from the living room and poured water into everyone's glasses.

Gina clasped her hands with excitement, when she saw the food offering. "Tomato, prosciutto, and fresh mozzarella salad," she exclaimed. "That was always a tradition at Christmas when Giovanni was growing up. We struggled then," she confided to the assembled gathering, "and prosciutto was always a luxury we just couldn't afford. It was such a special treat to have it at Christmas time. Isn't this nice, Mario? They've kept one of our traditions. Thank you, Rebecca. Thank you," she gushed.

"She likes to be called Becky, Mama," Giovanni corrected, seeing his wife with a wan smile, and knowing how she so disliked being addressed by her full name.

"You're serving meat and cheese on *these* dishes?" Esther inquired curtly, as Becky placed one in front of her mother.

"What's wrong with the plates? They look mighty fine to me." Mario picked up his fork and attacked the tomato.

Esther ignored him. "Where are the *milchediche* and *fleischediche* dishes?" she fumed.

"What in the world are *they?*" asked Mario.

"We have special plates for meat and dairy products. We eat dairy products on the milchediche dishes and meat on the fleishediche dishes," Jacob said matter-of-factly in his typical quiet, docile manner. "It's tradition."

Esther slapped her husband on the side of his leg to silence him. "Rebecca, you know we can't eat from these plates," she said.

"Mother, it won't kill you just this one time," Becky said firmly, wincing at being called Rebecca.

Giovanni rose from his seat. "Honey, it's not a problem. If your Mom and Dad want paper plates, we can do that." He removed the salad plates from Esther and Jacob and headed toward the kitchen.

Mario was bewildered. "Who cares about the dishes? So long as it tastes good. *Mangiamo!*" He threw his hands in the air, knife in one hand, fork in the other.

Esther ignored him. "Thank you, Giovanni. I am glad someone has respect for tradition."

"Esther," Jacob pleaded. "Don't be so harsh. It's nice to be here for the holiday." He turned to his daughter and patted her hand. "Thank you, princess."

Giovanni returned with the salad-filled paper plates and placed them in front of his in-laws.

Gina sensed the uncomfortable atmosphere, and even though she had planned to hold her thoughts on the decorations, she decided to try and relieve the tension. "Your table looks lovely, Becky." She was careful not to make the same mistake with her daughter-in-law's name twice. "Don't you agree, Mario?"

"Yes, that's some candlestick," boomed Mario. "Never seen one with nine candles before." He chuckled.

"That's a menorah," Jacob informed him. "It's one of our Hanukkah traditions."

"Why aren't they all lit?" Mario shrugged and looked questioningly around the table for a response.

"The holiday is spread over a period of days. We light one candle the first day, two the second and so on," chimed in Becky, totally ignoring her mother's behavior as Esther pushed the prosciutto to one side of her plate. *Fancy serving us cured ham at Hanukkah. Just like Rebecca to be so thoughtless and serve us something we can't eat.*

As if reading her mother's mind, and noticing the prosciutto on the edge of the plate, Becky spoke up. "You'll be pleased to know Ma, we're having brisket and potato pancakes for the main course."

Gina did a double take, while Mario, never one to keep his opinions to himself, complained "We're not having turkey? We always have turkey. It's *our* tradition. Why aren't *we* having turkey?"

"I'm sure the brisket will be delicious, dear." Gina patted her husband's hands in an attempt to placate him. *He never did know when to keep quiet.*

"Well, it's our tradition to have brisket at Hanukkah. I'm sure once you taste my brisket, you'll never want turkey again." Becky rose to collect the plates and kissed her father-in-law affectionately on the head.

Mario looked chastened.

"Don't worry, Pop, we have your favorite Italian Panetonne for dessert—home made."

"What? No challah bread pudding?" asked a surprised Jacob with uncharacteristic outrage.

Becky rounded the table and scooped up the paper plate in front of her father and gave him a gentle kiss on his head, too.

"Yes, Pa. There's bread pudding, too. We know how much you like it."

The phone rang in the kitchen. "I'll get it," she said fleeing to the kitchen. Becky nestled the phone between her ear and her shoulder and started removing the warm sliced brisket and potato pancakes, which were keeping warm in the oven.

"This is Father Mark Roades," said the voice at the other end of the line. "I would like to speak to Rebecca or Giovanni Largenti."

"This is Mrs. Largenti," replied Becky. "And I could use you over here right now, Father. I'm about to strangle someone, and may well need you to give the last rites," she quipped.

"Excuse me?" came the baffled reply.

"Never mind, Father. You've caught us in the middle of dinner. Can you call back, or can I call you?"

"Oh, I'm sorry. I'll be brief." He quickly explained the reason for his call.

"Well, I'll be darned. Five years, huh? Who would have guessed it? Sounds like a fun party. Let me speak to my husband, and see what he says. I'll call you back. I'm sure we'll be able to make it." She hung up and hurriedly continued putting the food into the serving dishes.

"Vanni, I need your help in the kitchen for a moment," she called.

"Why does she call you Vanni? What's wrong with Giovanni?" asked Gina.

It was now time for Giovanni to roll his eyes. He left the table and started for the kitchen. "It's just a term of endearment, Mama."

"Can you reach for some more paper plates for my folks, please?" Becky asked as she struggled with the tongs to stop the pancakes from breaking.

"Who was that on the phone?" Giovanni reached into the top of the cupboard.

"It was the minister from the chapel where we got married. Can you believe we'll have been married five years in January? That lady who worked there, I think he said her name was Rosemary. You remember … the one with the little dog. She's retiring the day of our anniversary, and they're holding a surprise party for her." She handed him the platter with the brisket and pancakes. "They're inviting all the couples who were married that day five years ago."

Carrying the vegetables, Becky followed her husband into the dining room. "I can't believe it's been five years," said Giovanni.

"What's been five years?" asked Esther inquisitively.

"Since we got married, Mother."

"If it's been five years, it's high time you gave us all some grandchildren," said Mario.

"I agree," said Jacob.

"That wasn't what you said before we got married, Dad," scoffed Becky. "You were more concerned about the faith in which the kids would be raised."

"I don't think you should speak to your father in that tone," snapped Esther.

"Well, as much as I would like grandchildren, I don't think it is really any of our business," Gina said timidly.

"Hold it folks," said Giovanni taking charge. "We're here to celebrate the holidays together as a family." He rose from his seat. Picking up the bottle of wine, he proceeded around the table pouring some into everyone's glass. "We're here to celebrate our joys, traditions, and health. Life is good for us all. Becky and I have been building up the salon. And as you know, she gave up her job at the Kabbalah Center."

"Thank God," muttered Esther.

"Becky is doing an outstanding job as general manager of the salon. She purchases all the products, does the bookkeeping, and hires and fires the staff when necessary. This allows me to style hair without being concerned with all those things," Giovanni continued.

"And a fine hair stylist you are, too," interjected Gina proudly.

Giovanni ignored his mother's comment. "Becky and I want a large family, and we'll have one in due course ... on our time schedule. Okay?"

Becky beamed proudly at him. "As always, my husband is right." She raised her glass. "Here's to family, here's to my husband, here's to love, and here's to life." She paused before proclaiming, "L'chaim! To life!"

Mario only understood one Hebrew word. "Mazeltov!" he ventured proudly, as he lifted his glass to meet his daughter-in-law's.

Jacob responded loudly, "Cheers!" He clinked his glass with that of Becky's.

Gina lifted her glass and smiled.

Esther stared at her half-filled glass as everyone looked for her to speak.

"If you want me to toast, you will need to fill this goblet to the top and stop being so stingy with the alcohol." Everyone round the table chuckled. "Now, pass the brisket," she demanded with a sense of fun. "And my daughter is right,

Mario. After you have tasted her home-cooked brisket, you'll never want turkey for Christmas again."

They all laughed heartily.

Becky looked lovingly at her husband, and blew him a discreet kiss across the table. Grinning, he returned the kiss, winked at her, and passed the brisket to his mother-in-law.

Chapter 5
A Life of Seclusion

Emmy was sitting in the comfort of her living room, enjoying the solitude of her elegant surroundings. So deeply engrossed in her mystery novel, the soothing classical music playing quietly in the background was almost ignored.

The sound of the phone ringing snapped her out of her whodunit world back to reality. *How irritating. Who would interrupt at such an inopportune time?*

"May I speak to Ruby Dixon?" came the man's mellow voice at the other end. Mark had been perplexed at only being able to locate the wife's name and phone number on the chapel's forms.

Instantly, Emmy was suspicious, and her protective shell was intuitively raised. Nobody who knew her called her Ruby. It was her birth name and only used by her parents.

"Who's this?" she demanded.

"My name is Father Mark Roades, and I'm calling from the Chapel of Eternal Love."

Emmy recalled her unhappy wedding day at the chapel, and realized immediately that she would have used her legal name when completing the forms. *What in the world could be prompting a call almost five years later?*

Even so, she relaxed a little and dropped her guard. Besides, she found the tone of the minister's voice pleasing.

"This is Ruby, but I prefer to be called Emmy. How can I help you?"

"I was actually planning to speak to you and your husband. You were married at my chapel almost five years ago." He was hoping to jog her memory, in case she had forgotten.

"As a matter of fact, we weren't. My marriage never took place," she responded flatly.

Mark immediately felt uncomfortable. "I'm so sorry to hear that, Miss Dixon."

"I was actually stood up, Father Roades. My would-be-husband was a complete no show."

He detected a certain bitterness in the tone of her voice and was acutely embarrassed. "I'm extremely sorry, Miss Dixon. Truly, it must have been devastating."

"Oh please, call me Emmy. It *was* a tough blow at the time, but one survives. I picked up the pieces and carried on, as we all do."

"Hopefully, you received a lot of support from friends and family."

Emmy chuckled forlornly. "Father Roades, I don't have any family to speak of. At least, none who choose to acknowledge me. And I soon discovered in my line of work, one does not have any real friends, either. Everyone is very cold, calculating, and devious."

"What line of work are you in, if you don't mind my asking?" he inquired innocently.

Emmy paused and lit a cigarette. "I happened to have run the most exclusive escort agency in Las Vegas," she responded candidly. The other end of the phone went quiet. "Does that shock you, Father?"

"Nothing shocks me, Emmy," he replied. "We're both in professions where nothing should shock us."

There are things that have shocked me, and I'm certain would have stunned this clergyman, Emmy thought, as she contemplated some of the individuals she had encountered over the years. But she was not of the mind to enlighten him. "I'm sure you're right," she responded.

"You mentioned that you *happened* to run the agency, as if it were in the past?"

"I sold it, Father. After the marriage fell through, I went through an entire gamut of emotions—anger, pain, hate, bitterness, and sadness. You name it. I felt it. I finally sold the business for a handsome sum and spent the next couple of years traveling around the world. I visited some of the most exotic and fascinating places on the planet." She paused, before adding, "But one cannot escape loneliness."

Mark listened to her sad tale and felt a sense of compassion toward this survivor.

"What do you do now?"

"Not much of anything. Life is actually very boring. I've become quite a recluse. The grand, fast-paced life no longer appeals to me, Father. And as you can imagine, it's not easy finding a job when your entire career has been in a questionable and frowned-upon profession." She exhaled her cigarette forming a couple of smoke rings and flicked the ash in the nearby crystal ashtray. She found him quite refreshing and enjoyed talking with someone who she assumed had no ulterior motive. "But to what do I owe the call? I'm sure you didn't contact me to hear my tale of woe. My five year old check to the chapel didn't bounce, did it?" she asked drily, hoping to add a touch of humor to the conversation.

He laughed. "Not at all. Well, not that I'm aware of anyway. But then I've only been at the chapel for three years." He went on to explain the purpose for his call and the surprise party for Rosemary.

"Of course I remember Rosemary. She was an angel of mercy that day. I don't know how I would have made it without her comforting spirit. I recall her loveable little dog, too, whining constantly as if he knew something was wrong. He was certainly right. Normally, I would decline an invite like this, but I owe it to Rosemary to attend. I was a total stranger, but she sure was a friend that day when I needed one most."

Mark was touched by Emmy's compassionate recollection, and was in awe that Rosemary had clearly touched the lives of so many people in so many different ways. "That's good," he replied. "I'll add your name to the list and will contact you with the specifics nearer the time."

"If there's anything I can do to help, Father, please contact me."

A thought suddenly flashed through Mark's mind. He had been listening intently to Emmy. "As a matter of fact, there *is* something. I am looking for a replacement for Rosemary and have not had much success. Would you ever consider coming to work at the chapel as office manager and wedding organizer?"

Emmy started to laugh uncontrollably. "You can't be serious Father Roades. That's an absurd notion. Why, it's totally preposterous," she said, stubbing out her cigarette.

"Is it? You have all the attributes for the job. You obviously have business acumen, so you would be capable of handling all the office requirements. Your telephone demeanor is calm and reassuring—an absolute must for a wedding chapel. You also are caring and compassionate, given your acknowledgement of Rosemary's assistance to you during your time of distress. Finally, you have a good memory for names. I only mentioned my name once, and you remembered it. The only issue I can think of is, we would probably not be able to pay you the money you are probably worth on the market."

"This conversation is absolutely ludicrous. Imagine me, former owner of an escort agency working for a minister in a wedding chapel."

"Well, as the proverb says, 'The Lord works in mysterious ways'. By your own admission, your life is boring. Will you at least consider it?"

Emmy paused for a moment, finally realizing he was serious. "Okay, Father. I'll think about it," she said slowly, suddenly considering his offer for the first time.

Mark was relieved. "Well, if you're earnestly thinking about it, the first thing you can do is start calling me Mark."

"Alright, Mark. Anything else?"

"Yes. There's an elderly couple by the name of Windmeyer. The gentleman is in memory care, and his wife doesn't drive. She said she would think about coming to the party. I'm trying to coax her to attend, but she'll need someone to pick her up. Could you do that for me?"

"I believe I know the couple you are referring to, Father Roades ... sorry, Mark. I think they might have been the couple ahead of me that day." Emmy was dismayed to learn that her former client, Oscar Windmeyer, with whom she had a brief liaison, was in a memory care facility. She was not about to divulge she knew Oscar personally. Those details would always be kept private. "I'd be delighted to pick up Mrs. Windmeyer."

"I've a feeling we are going to be quite a team, Emmy."

"Now, you're getting ahead of yourself, Mark," she chided gently. "I only said I would *consider* the position. I would need to know a lot more about it. Besides, how would I get trained? Rosemary would have to show me the ropes. She is certain to remember me, and how would you and I explain our meeting? She would surely know it is not a job for which I would apply."

"Minor details," Mark responded. "Give the idea some thought. If you want to know more, perhaps we can chat about it over coffee one morning."

"Perhaps," she replied.

"By the way, did you ever find out why your would-be-husband never showed up? Or do you not want to talk about it?"

"Dexter? No, I never did discover why. He refused to accept my calls. I wrote to him, but he never responded. I surmised he went back to his wife. He was not one to live alone and went through a lot of guilt when they divorced. Sorry, but he was a bastard for what he did to me. I'll never forgive him for it."

"But you must forgive him," preached Mark.

"No lectures, please," she responded. "I'll think about your offer, Okay?"

"Alright," he said quietly.

After they hung up, Emmy immediately picked up her book and tried to immerse herself in it, but found she was reading the same page over and over. *Damn!* She slammed the book down on the table. Unable to focus and concentrate, she ran her hands through her still wavy mane of red hair as all the memories of her past with Dexter came flooding back. She rose from her chair, headed toward the bar, and poured her favorite imported French red wine into a finely-cut, Waterford crystal glass. Returning to the chair, Emmy lifted her feet onto the small ottoman, lit another cigarette, and took a sip of the wine. Laying her head back on the chair, she stared at the ceiling, once again pondering her future.

Truth was, despite everything, she was still in love with Dexter. And she knew it.

Chapter 6
Double Correction

Lester picked up the phone from the bedroom extension in the left wing of the house. At the same time, his twin brother, Chester, lifted the receiver from the cradle in his bedroom in the right wing.

"Hello," they both said simultaneously with a cheerful tone.

Mark Roades had already deduced from the paperwork that there were two sets of twins involved in this marriage. "I'd like to speak to Lester and Dolly Roscoe or Chester and Molly Roscoe."

"You're speaking to Lester Roscoe."

"As well has his brother Chester," chimed in the other twin.

Mark started his now familiar patter explaining the reason for his call.

"We just thought it would be a fitting farewell to Rosemary if all the people who were married five years to the day could attend. It would mean a lot to Rosemary, I'm sure."

"Well, we won't have been married for five years to the day, Father," said Lester.

"No, not at all, sir. You're quite wrong there," followed Chester.

Mark frowned, as he looked at the documents in front of him. Had he erred?

"Hmmm. According to my records here … ."

"Sorry to interrupt you Father, but your records are correct even though they're wrong, if you know what I mean." It was one of the rare times Chester was able to get ahead of Lester in a conversation.

"I'm afraid I *don't* know what you mean. I'm confused," responded Mark.

"I'm no longer married to Dolly," said Lester.

"And I'm no longer married to Molly," added Chester.

"Oh, I'm sorry to hear that," said Mark. *What a pity. These gents seem real friendly and affable.*

"Don't be. We're not," continued Chester. "We simply married the wrong women. Don't ask how or why or what. None of us could put our fingers on it. Dolly and Molly are also twins."

"What my brother is trying to tell you is that something wasn't quite right when we married Dolly and Molly. It took us most of a year to figure it out," said Lester. "Once we did, it was easy. I divorced Dolly, and Chester divorced Molly. It was the right thing to do."

"Then, I married Dolly and Lester married Molly. That was just over four years ago."

I've heard of some unique situations, but this one takes the cake, thought Mark Roades. It was one of the rare occasions he was at a loss for words. All he could muster was, "So are you all happy now?"

"Absolutely, we're happy," commented Lester.

"Definitely," added Chester. "I know the church doesn't

approve of divorce, but we simply made a mistake which we rectified. We all love each other and we're happy. That's all that matters, isn't it?"

"Yes, it's all about love, Father. Our marriages are all about love," said Lester.

Hard to argue that point, pondered the minister. "Well, I don't think the remarriage should disqualify you from attending Rosemary's farewell party. I'd love for you to attend all the same. I'm sure she'll still remember you."

"Oh, she does. She was there when we married at the chapel the second time round. Both she and her dog were just as confused by the second marriage as they were the first." Lester laughed heartily. "I still recall her little dog running round and round in circles, from one foot to the other. I think she called him Buster."

"Lester, we'll need to check our work schedules," noted his brother solemnly. "We're both card dealers in the high-roller section of a casino here in town, Father. It depends on what shifts we have that day."

"You're right, of course, Chester. At least, we don't have to worry about Dolly and Molly's jobs anymore."

"Do they work daytime?" asked the minister.

"Oh no, they used to work at the box office of one of the showrooms, but they gave up their jobs to become stay at home moms when we had children," Lester replied. "We'll need to check and see if we can find a babysitter, too, brother."

"Oh, so you're proud parents now?" inquired Mark.

"Both of us are. We each have one child. We were all hoping for twins, but are just thankful the children were born healthy," commented Lester.

"Lester and Molly have a little boy, and Dolly and I have a little girl who was born two days later. They're six months old."

Father Roades smiled.

"Molly and I christened our son, Chester, in honor of my brother."

"And Dolly and I named our daughter, Molly, in honor of my sister-in-law. Less names to remember and less confusing for everyone."

Personally, I can't imagine anything more confusing, thought the clergyman as he tried to imagine life in their household. Still, he could not deny that the two men with whom he was conversing seemed genuine, caring, and loving husbands and fathers.

Chester continued, "And next time round, if there's a girl, she'll be called Dolly, and the boy will be called Lester."

"What if you both have the twins that you hope for? What names will you give them?" asked the minister.

The twins were momentarily pensive as if considering the possibility for the first time. "I guess we'll just cross that bridge when we come to it," offered Lester lamely.

The sound of a car pulling into the driveway could be heard.

There was a pause, and then one of the twins said, "Must run, Father. Our wives have just returned from shopping with the kids. Give us your phone number, and we'll get back to you as soon as we know our schedule and whether we can find a baby-sitter."

"Sounds good," said Mark, as he recited his cell phone number. "You will be receiving a formal invite though from the Bella Del Mundo. I enjoyed talking with you both and wish you all a Merry Christmas with your loved ones."

"Same to you, Father," said Lester.

"And to Rosemary, as well," added Chester.

"By the way, please be certain and let your wives know that it *is* a surprise party for Rosemary. So, when you call back, in the unlikely event she answers my phone, be sure not to let on."

"Got it," the twins replied in unison and hung up.

Mark determined he would make one more call for the day. He had made a good start and was pleased with the positive and enthusiastic response from all the people with whom he had connected so far.

Chester and Lester rushed out to greet their wives and remove Chester and Molly from their baby seats in the car. They hugged the little ones as they brought them indoors, and kissed their wives; Lester kissing Molly on the left cheek and Chester kissing Dolly on the right.

As they unpacked their provisions in the kitchen, Molly and Dolly chatted incessantly about their escapades in the shopping malls and how crazy it had been at the supermarket. Finally, with the groceries unpacked, they all moved into the family room, placed the youngsters in high-chairs, and sat down; the women still prattling on. It was a while before Lester and Chester could tell them of their invite to the party.

"We can't possible attend. We have absolutely nothing to wear," declared Molly.

"Nothing at all," nodded Dolly. "Well, nothing suitable anyway. Must say though, it would be really nice to attend a function at the swanky, new Bella Del Mundo. They say it's fabulous. Wonder if the owner and her dishy-looking husband will be there. She's old enough to be his mother, you know."

"Where do you see or read all this stuff?" asked an exasperated Lester, raising his left hand.

"Their pictures are always in the newspapers, donating money to some charity or attending some gala event, dear husband of mine."

"Who cares?" asked Chester, throwing his right arm in the air. "Point is, if our work schedules permit, are we going or aren't we? You have plenty of time to *make* something to wear."

"Not with Christmas around the corner we won't." Dolly was shaking her head.

"What if Chester and my Christmas gifts to you both were to *buy* yourself new dresses?"

"Now you're talking." Dolly leaned over and gave her husband a big kiss on the cheek. Her face lit up. "Molly, I know exactly what we can get to wear." She embraced her husband. "You might also have to apply to the Bella Del Mundo for a new job, to pay for these outfits," she quipped.

"Might not be such a bad idea anyway. Haven't had a raise for the last two years. Maybe it is time to look around," said Lester.

All four adults looked at each other in contemplation.

Chester and Molly junior began to cry in their high chairs.

"Time for dinner," called Molly, as she rose from her seat and headed toward the kitchen, followed by Dolly. Chester and Lester picked up their children and started setting the dinner table; Lester holding baby Chester with his left arm, and Chester holding baby Molly in his right. The babies chuckled and gurgled as they clutched their daddy's shirts.

Chapter 7

Love Hawaiian Style

Mark looked at the papers of the next couple he was about to call—male listed as residing in Hawaii and female listed in New York. *How in the world did these two meet?* he mused. Since it was midafternoon Hawaiian time and well into the evening in Manhattan, he took a chance to see if the Hawaiian phone number was still active and dialed it.

Julian stopped rearranging the flower display in the windows of his Waikiki florist shop when the phone rang. He picked it up just before the call went to the answering machine. "*Mele Kalikimaka* and Merry Christmas from Awesome Orchids of Oahu. This is Julian speaking."

Mark was pleased he had obviously made the correct contact. He introduced himself and inquired as to whether Julian remembered the wedding chapel.

"Of course, I remember the Chapel of Eternal Love. I picked it because of its name. Eternal love is what I promised my wife. Our wedding day was the happiest day of my life, Father. I sure hope it meant something to my wife," he chuckled. "There was something very magical about the chapel, and we remember Rosemary and her dog fondly. Rosemary played the piano at our wedding, as we had a baritone sing the theme song from *An Affair to Remember*." The movie reference was lost on Mark. "When I recall that day, I can still hear

Rosemary's beautiful playing. We send her a Christmas card each year. How is she? And how's the little dog?"

"Well, I am glad you haven't forgotten Rosemary because she's the reason for my call." He proceeded to inform Julian of the pending retirement and the surprise party.

Julian was excited. "Father, how magnificent! You've just given me a marvelous idea. I knew our fifth anniversary was coming up and have been wondering what I could do to surprise Hayley—that's my wife. You've provided the perfect solution—a return to Las Vegas. We first met there, at the restaurant at the top of the Stratosphere. By the way, is it still there?"

"Yes, the Stratosphere is still there. I wouldn't know about the restaurant. Fine dining is not in a minister's budget," Father Roades joked. "I was wondering though, how you and your wife met given your geographical residences at the time."

"It's a long story, Father. To make it short, we met on the Internet. We're both romantics at heart. Six months after corresponding, we decided to meet approximately half-way. Las Vegas fit the bill. We returned there six months later and married at the chapel. Our wedding was a year to the day since we'd exchanged our first emails. We're both interested in nature. Hayley, at the time, worked for a florist in New York. She's now part of the family business here in Hawaii. We have some orchid farms and a couple of flower shops. We haven't returned to the mainland since we moved here, so it will be a nice break and very romantic to return to where it all started. Certainly, it will be nice to revisit the chapel."

"Good. Then I can put you down for two attending?"

"Absolutely," responded Julian, still flush with excitement

over his planned surprise. "We'd love to be a part of the festivities. By the way, if you need to call back and Hayley answers the phone be sure not to say anything. It needs to be our secret."

"Well, it's safe with me," laughed Father Mark. They hung up after the details of the event were shared and noted.

Julian quickly dialed the Honolulu store.

"Mama, I need you and Dad to do me a favor. I need you to look after Jasmine for Hayley and me."

"Not a problem," she replied. "What grandmother doesn't love the opportunity to spend time with her favorite granddaughter?"

"She's your *only* granddaughter, Mama."

"But she's still my favorite." There was a joyous tone in her lilt. "What day and what time?"

"Actually, it needs to be for a few days, Mama. I'm taking Hayley to the mainland."

"In her condition? Is something wrong? What's the matter?" Her voice changed to one of concern.

"Nothing's the matter, Mama. And Hayley's only four months pregnant. It's not as if she's going into labor."

"Hopefully, this time she will give birth to a boy, who will grow up to be just as handsome as his father and his grandfather." Julian's mother opened her locket and looked at the photo inside with her husband and son together at Julian's graduation. *How alike they look with their dark complexions, dimples, and cleft chins.*

"Mama, stop. We just want the baby healthy like Jasmine."

"I know. But it would sure make your papa happy. When do you want us to look after Jasmine?"

"In the new year. I want to surprise Hayley and fly to Las Vegas for a few days to celebrate our fifth wedding anniversary."

"The wedding to which we weren't invited?" Her voice now turned icy.

"Mama, let's not go through *that* again." He rolled his eyes in exasperation. "The lady who played the piano at our ceremony is retiring. They're having a party for her. I thought it would be nice to go back to where Hayley and I first met. You can understand that can't you, Mama?"

She thought for a moment. She had never been one to be angry with her son. "Of course, we'll look after Jasmine. Your papa will take care of the Waikiki store for you while you're gone. I'll hold down the fort for you here. How about you and Hayley coming over for some dinner this evening? Your father's cooking."

"Would love to, Mama. But Hayley is packing a picnic. We're driving along the coast and will watch the sun go down. It's been a beautiful day, and the sunset should be spectacular. Here she is now. I see her driving into the parking lot. Gotta go. Love you. And love to Papa. Remember it's a secret." He hung up. His mother shook her head.

Hayley walked into the shop. Releasing the hand of her four-year-old daughter, she said, "Go give your daddy a big kiss and a hug."

Jasmine ran toward Julian with her arms outstretched. "Daddy!" she cried. Her face beamed, revealing the same dimples she had inherited from her father. He scooped her up in his arms and swirled her around before giving her a big kiss.

"And how's my princess today? Were you a good girl at the care center?"

"She was very well-behaved," Hayley responded. "Mrs. Marks said she is the perfect child and wishes all the children in her care would be like Jasmine."

"Must take after her mother," smiled Julian. He reached out with his other arm to hug his wife. His mind was still fresh from the vivid memories recalled during his conversation with Father Mark. He looked at Hayley and marveled at how beautiful and how unchanged she still was. It was as if time had stood still.

"Why are you looking at me like that?" she asked.

"Like what?" Julian snapped back to reality. "I'm sorry, darling. I was just thinking." He returned Jasmine to the floor.

"Daddy, are we going soon?"

"Yes, sweetheart. I just need to lock up the shop, and then, we're on our way. Is Baxter in the car?"

"Yes, he's lying down in the back of the SUV," said Hayley. "I had to take him to the vet this afternoon. Baxter needs to lose a few pounds. The vet said he is too heavy, even for a five-year-old St. Bernard. We need to start taking him for those evening walks again."

Jasmine ran out to the car, as Julian switched off the lights, and turned the "open" sign to reflect "closed". Hayley removed all the money from the cash register and placed it in a zipped bag before securing it in the safe. "I'll do the deposit tomorrow," she said.

They were soon driving along the coast—the ocean on one side and a mixture of mother nature's frangipani and palm trees on the other. There was surprisingly little traffic. Hayley felt the humidity through the open windows and couldn't wait until they arrived at their destination. Jasmine chattered incessantly about her day, while both parents smiled, listening intently to her innocent and child-like observations.

Arriving at their selected location, they opened the rear door, and Baxter immediately tore off down the beach barking effusively.

"Wait for me, Baxter. Wait for me," yelled Jasmine as she ran after him.

The beach was deserted, and the only sound was that of the ocean as the small waves crashed gently to the sandy shore. Julian locked the car. He and Hayley walked slowly, hand in hand, in the direction Jasmine and Baxter had headed. They could see their dog and watched him turn around and race back toward Jasmine, who sat down and started to build a sandcastle.

Julian asked Hayley in a soft tone. "Are you happy?"

She was taken aback. "Well, that's an odd question … so out of the blue."

"I just wondered. I was thinking of how you had to make all the adjustments and sacrifices when we married. You gave up your exciting and fast-paced life in New York and have had to adjust to one on an island way out here in the Pacific Ocean. I was born here. I've never even asked if you felt "island fever" that many seem to complain about."

She pulled him toward her, put her arms around his neck, and looked into his deep brown eyes that she loved so much. "How could I not be happy? I live in a wonderful home overlooking the ocean and have loving in-laws. And I work in a terrific shop surrounded by beautiful orchids, which are my passion. It is a continuous joy to tend to them every day. I have an amazing daughter and am married to the most loving, tender, and handsome man on the planet who happens to be the best father in the whole wide world." She kissed him gently on the lips. He placed his arms tenderly around his wife and turned her kiss into a penetrating and passionate one.

Their embrace was interrupted by shouts of "Mummy, Daddy. Come look at my sandcastle." As they sauntered along toward Jasmine, Julian picked up a seashell and carved a heart in the sand. Baxter continued to run up and down the shoreline with his happy bark. Both marveled at their daughter's masterpiece and led her back toward the car, where they removed a blanket and the picnic basket. Hayley laid out the supper handing a chicken salad sandwich and pineapple juice to Jasmine, while placing crackers with brie cheese, pâté, and some stuffed mushrooms on plates for Julian and herself. Julian popped open the sparkling white wine and poured a glass for each of them. They savored the meal slowly, absorbing the surroundings. The silhouette of a horse rider trotting by the water's edge in the distance briefly interrupted the tranquility. Jasmine yawned, which signaled to Hayley she was ready for bed. They laid her down on the wide back seat of the car and covered her with blankets. Her little head had hardly touched the pillow before she was asleep. Baxter jumped into the back of the SUV and curled up as if he was Jasmine's custodian.

The sun was sinking, and it was very still and quiet. Julian filled their glasses with more wine and put his arm around his wife, as the two of them lovingly watched the sun slowly disappear below the horizon.

Chapter 8

A Change of Hearts

As the new day started, Mark hoped to continue his string of successful phone calls, when he hit his first stumbling block. *Looks like I'm going to need the Nelson's private eye,* and dialed the number.

Chad answered his cell phone. "Bella Del Mundo Hotel and Resort, this is Chad Nelson speaking."

"Morning, Mr. Nelson. This is Mark Roades from the Chapel of Eternal Love."

"Ah yes, Father. Say, I haven't had time yet to follow through on the couple you wanted me to track down for you."

"Not a problem. I hardly expected a response so soon. It was only yesterday I mentioned them to you. I was actually calling to see if you could have your private eye seek another couple for me. I'm having trouble locating a Kurt Maxwell and Kathleen Rogers. I just have his address as Iraq and hers as Minneapolis, Minnesota. Kathleen's phone number is the only one listed on the papers, and it is disconnected. Directory assistance has no record of her in Minneapolis."

"Oh, Father," Chad exclaimed. "I don't even have to go to our P. I. for that one. It's too much of a coincidence for it not to be Congresswoman Maxwell-Rogers."

"A congresswoman?" Mark wondered why she would have been marrying in Las Vegas.

"I think so," said Chad. "Let me do a Google search on my computer. I remember seeing a special about her on TV just before the last election. She used to be an anti-war activist, and now, seems to be championing further funding for the military in order to put more troops on the ground in Iraq." He paused as he keyed the computer. "Yup. There she is. Kathleen Maxwell-Rogers, congresswoman from Texas. Born in Minnesota. Husband is listed as an attorney. Here's the number to her office in Washington D.C."

"That's fantastic! With your help I've overcome my first hurdle for the day."

"Pleased I've been able to help. How are you coming along so far with contacting the rest of the people?"

"Very well. I've made quite a few contacts and am pleased to say that all the couples are still married that I've spoken to. So far, they're all probably attending with the exception of one, who I'm trying to persuade into coming." He thought sadly of poor Sarah and her plight with her husband in the memory care facility. "How is Mrs. Nelson?"

"Please, Father. We will be speaking to each other often during the next couple of weeks. The names are Chad and Pru. But now you must forgive me, I have a staff meeting which I am late for, so I must go. Maybe we can chat again soon?"

"Of course. Thanks for your help, Chad."

On hanging up, Mark immediately placed a call to the DC office of Congresswoman Kathleen Maxwell-Rogers, which was answered by a staff member.

"I'm sorry the congresswoman is on the House floor at the moment. Can I help you, sir?"

"Unfortunately not. I really need to speak to the congresswoman. Perhaps you could ask her to call Father Mark Roades at the Chapel of Eternal Love in Las Vegas? Let me give you my number."

Las Vegas? thought the intern. *What connection would the congresswoman have with a minister in Las Vegas?* She scribbled the information on her message pad. "I'll be sure to let her know you called. I don't know if she'll have time to contact you today. She's a member of the Armed Services Committee, as well as the Foreign Affairs Committee. They both meet this afternoon."

"Whenever she can call me, it will be greatly appreciated. Thanks for your help."

After they hung up, Mark started to think about how Chad had used Google and decided that could assist him as well, with locating some of the remaining couples. He became so engrossed in his research he was startled when his cell phone rang.

"This is Congresswoman Kathleen Maxwell-Rogers calling for Mark Roades."

"This is he, and I thank you for returning my call." He congratulated her on her election, and enquired as to whether it was she who married at the chapel five years earlier.

"Yes, that was my husband and I. Congratulations to you too, Father, for tracking me down. It could not have been easy. My husband was serving in Iraq at the time, and did not want to list his parents address on the forms. I think he just listed Iraq as his residence." She laughed gently.

"Be sure and thank him for his service."

"Don't say that to him. He paid a very high price. Unfortunately, he was carrying a sick child to one of our hospitals there, and a bomb exploded. It cost my husband his right leg."

"I am saddened to hear that, congresswoman. Does he feel bitter about it?"

"No, not bitter. I'm the one who's bitter. He was angry. Angry at his government for sending him there."

"Oh? Forgive me. I understood you were in favor of sending more troops to Iraq."

"I am, Father. My husband and I have totally switched positions. I used to be against the war, but now I want to punish those murderers for their cruel acts. Not only did my husband lose a leg, I lost my brother, Brian, who was Kurt's best friend. I've seen the emotional and physical effect it has had on my husband. Kurt used to feel the war was being waged for an honorable cause. Now, he feels it all could have been avoided. If it had, he would still have both his legs."

"Well, I suppose sometimes war isn't always the answer, congresswoman."

"And sometimes war is the *only* answer, Father. I said goodbye to my husband at McCarran Airport the day after our wedding in Las Vegas. He looked so smart and so proud in his military uniform, sporting his medals. The next time I saw and greeted him at the Dallas airport in Texas, he was on crutches."

Mark detected the passion and terseness, as well as the forlorn and bitter tone. He decided not to pursue the line of conversation and segued into the purpose of his call.

"That sounds like a very nice gesture, Father. I remember Rosemary and her dog well. Congress will have just returned from the winter break, so my husband and I would have to meet in Las Vegas. Not sure if he would make the trip by himself, but I'll call him and find out. I have your number, so either he or I will get back to you. It will probably be Kurt. I have just enough time to call him and grab a quick lunch before making it to my committee meetings this afternoon. Appreciate your efforts in finding us, Father."

"And thank you for your time, too, congresswoman. I hope you can both make it. You will be receiving a formal invite from the Bella Del Mundo."

Kathleen replaced the receiver and sat for a moment, tapping her pencil on the desk. The conversation had rekindled the joy of her wedding day and how plane delays nearly jettisoned the most special day of her life. She relived the moment when she met Kurt at the chapel; the memory of his passionate and tender kiss as he held her in his strong arms, suddenly engulfed her once again.

She used her private cell phone to call him.

Kurt answered in his Texas drawl, "Hi, honey. It's unusual for you to call me in the middle of the day." He had been reading the highlights of the previous evening's Dallas Cowboys' game, and now he put down the newspaper. "What's up?"

Kathleen relayed her conversation with Father Roades. "The conversation brought back wonderful memories of our wedding day," she said.

"Yeah, that was a great little chapel you found. Remember how that little dog sat to attention when we said our vows?

His nose was in the air, tail outstretched." He chuckled.

Kathleen became serious. "I'd really like to go to this, Kurt. It's important to me."

"Why?" Her tone was not lost on him. "I didn't know that lady meant so much to you."

"She does. I'll never forget how she came through for me that day. You remember I was late because of the plane changes and missed connections? She made a little bridal bouquet for me, helped me with my hair, and out of my rumpled clothes into my wedding outfit. I was so flustered ..."

"You, flustered?" Kurt interjected. He started to laugh.

"Yes, I was a mess. Flustered and nervous. Rosemary was like an angel from heaven that morning. I wanted the day to be perfect."

"It *was* perfect."

"I know. But it was Rosemary who made it so."

"And the little dog." Kurt laughed again, and then thought for a moment. "But how will you manage it? You'll be in Washington. It's just after the start of the new session."

"I can catch the red eye. You could fly in from Texas. It would be just like our wedding day."

"Except this time I will fly in with one leg. Last time, I was a whole man."

Kathleen stopped him. "Don't. Please don't torture yourself. Besides, I thought you weren't going to wallow in self pity."

"Sorry. You're right. A momentary lapse."

She deftly changed the subject. "How are things at work today?"

"You know something, honey?" He leaned forward on his

desk. "I'm so glad I didn't go into the family law practice. I know Dad was disappointed, but I just feel so much happier opening this placement center for our veterans. It's heartwarming seeing them walk in here. Some with all kinds of handicaps, some still suffering from Post Traumatic Stress Disorder, but all wanting to get back to their lives and find jobs. They're an inspiration. Sometimes, I can give them legal advice, too. It's rewarding when I find all these companies willing to hire our veterans, and even occasionally *create* positions for them. They remind me of how blessed I am to have come home, especially to have come home to you."

Kathleen glowed with pride at her husband. "Darling, I love you, and I am so proud of you and what you're trying to accomplish."

"I'm so very proud of you too, sweetheart. I love you so much, even though I wish you were on the Veterans Affairs Committee and not the Armed Services and Foreign Affairs," he teased.

She laughed. "I'll see what I can do next session. So, are we going to go to Las Vegas?"

"If that's what you want. It will be nice to see the chapel again."

"Here's the number for the minister. Please give him a call this afternoon. I'm going for a quick snack and then off to my meetings. Bye, honey. Love you. Oh, he'll need our address. They're sending out formal invites. Give him the home one, I'll never get it here in Washington."

"Love you, too. I'm heading out to my monthly Veterans of Foreign Wars meeting this afternoon."

Kathleen picked up the photograph of her brother, Brian,

from her office desk. It was the same photo she carried in her suitcase to her wedding. She gently and tenderly waved her fingers over the picture. She was very bitter when he died in Iraq, but coped with it over the years by realizing were it not for his service in the army, she would never had met Kurt. "Thank you for steering my wonderful husband into my life," she said aloud, looking at her brother's face. "He is the greatest gift you could have given me."

Kathleen kissed her fingertips and placed them over the smile looking at her from the photograph, before replacing it on her desk. She picked up her purse and headed out to lunch.

Chapter 9
Still the King

"Elvis Online Memorabilia. Please hold," chirped Cilla in her southern drawl.

Mark wondered whether he had dialed the correct number, as he listened to the sounds of Elvis crooning "Blue Christmas" over the telephone line. The song finished and immediately segued into the King's rendition of "I'll Be Home for Christmas Day." He was about to hang up when the female voice returned.

"I'm sorry to keep you waiting, this is Cilla speaking. How can I help you?"

"My name is Father Mark Roades, and I'm calling from the Chapel of Eternal Love in Las Vegas." He paused to see if there would be an immediate response or recognition.

"Gosh, darn!" she exclaimed. "My husband and I married there almost five years ago. And both of our parents wed there, too. They had a double ceremony thirty-five years ago on the same date as Elvis's and mine. Then, would you believe, they actually renewed their vows when Elvis and I said ours? Isn't that a kick?"

Mark smiled. *What a bubbly and effervescent personality this lady has. I can see why they have her answering the phone.* He glanced down at the three wedding forms Rosemary had clipped together, and suddenly, the trio of ceremonies that day made sense.

"Say, is that Elvis impersonator, Kid Galahad, still around?" Cilla prattled on, barely pausing. "He sure was something else. It could have been Elvis in the flesh. He was fantastic. Absolutely made our wedding day, he did. Hey, and what about the little dog? Is he still at the chapel? We could hear him howling away in the office, as Elvis crooned to us. What a cute little *hound dog*," she giggled. "I'm sorry, Father. We tend to talk in Elvis lingo around here. "Hound Dog" was the name of one of Elvis' biggest hit songs. I meant that little dachshund was cute."

"Oh yes, Buster is still alive and well. As for Kid Galahad, I am not up on those things. Rosemary handles all that. She is more in touch with that facet of our weddings than I am," he said, trying to conceal his disdain. "In fact, Rosemary is the purpose for my call."

"I'm sorry. I am so surprised to hear from you and so excited at all the memories of my wedding day that have come flooding back, I almost forgot *you* contacted me. What can I do for you?"

Mark explained the purpose for his call.

"Aw, shucks. It sounds like a swell idea. I'm not sure if we can make it happen, though. You see, we all run a family business here. We collect and sell Elvis Presley memorabilia. My Dad and Bobby, that's my father-in-law, travel the country and all around the world seeing what they can pick up at estate sales, souvenir shops, and antique stores ..."

"Antique stores?" Mark interjected.

"Sure. In certain parts of the country and the globe, anything over twenty years is considered antique." She giggled some more. "My mother schedules all the trips for Dad and Bobby, does all the bookkeeping, and controls the inventory. Mavis, my mother-in-law, handles all the online orders and scours the internet for rare Elvis items. My husband, Elvis, packs and ships all the orders from our warehouse at the back of our office suite, and we just hope we don't get anything back saying *return to sender.*" She chuckled at her own joke. "Sorry, Father. I couldn't resist that one. My job is to answer the phones and email correspondence for special requests and orders, between fulfilling my role as mother to my adorable twin girls, Lisa and Marie. I work from home. It's a full time operation, that's for sure. We barely have time to make it to church on Sundays." She was now laughing loudly.

Mark smiled on hearing Cilla's infectious laugh. "So you're the official Elvis Presley Fan Club?"

"Oh, hell no," said Cilla. "Oops, I'm sorry Father. I shouldn't have said that, should I?"

"I'm sure God will forgive you," said Mark.

"Oh, good. No, we're small meat and potatoes compared to the real fan club. They are a huge operation. We're just the small fry. We do fill a niche, though, as we will look for those rare and hard to find items for the devout collector. We've picked up some unusual mementos in some very strange places throughout the world. I'll need to check and see if everyone's schedules can be arranged in order to go back to Vegas. Say, I'll try and get the whole family on a conference call after we hang up, and I'll call you back? Does that work for you?"

"Yes, it sure works for me," he said in a gentle manner. "Although, you can just respond to the formal invite when you receive it."

"Okay. Oops, gotta' go. The other phone is ringing. Y'all be sure and have a nice day out there, ya hear? Say hi to Rosemary. I'm sure she can't have forgotten us."

I'm certain of that, thought Mark, as he hung up, laughing to himself at her slang.

Cilla could barely contain her excitement. She hastily made some grits for Lisa and Marie's lunch and immediately called the business. "Mavis, can you get Val and Elvis into your office and see if you can get Bobby and Dad on the line, then put me on the speaker phone?"

"What's up?" Mavis responded. "Nothing wrong with the girls is there?"

"No, please just get everyone into the office. I have some exciting news."

"Honey, why are you so *all shook up?*" inquired Elvis loudly as he entered the room, throwing his body into the armchair.

"*Tutti frutti,* are you expecting again?" asked Val, who hurried into Mavis's office.

"We're all here and I have Bobby and Mike on the line," announced Mavis.

"Oh my *flaming star,*" said Val as Cilla relayed all the details of her conversation with the minister from the chapel. "Must say, I don't remember Rosemary too well, other than that she was a sweet soul, but I do remember that little dog. I think it would be a heap of fun to go back to Las Vegas for our thirty-fifth wedding anniversary, and you two kids could celebrate your fifth. You know, we could do it *for ole' times sake.*"

"Yeah, I kind of have a *burning love* to visit sin city again," concurred Mavis.

They all chimed in, trying to work out the logistics of making it happen, each one talking over the other—but all excited at the possibility of returning to Las Vegas. There were the travel schedules to consider, whether to place Lisa and Marie with other family members or be part of the trip, and whether to fly or drive. After much deliberation, Mavis took charge.

"Okay, listen up, ya'll. The party is on Friday. And Bobby, you're scheduled to be in Phoenix for an auction the Tuesday before. So, you do that, then go to Tucson on Wednesday and see if there's anything to buy. The next day, go to Vegas and scour the stores around the strip." Mavis caught her breath and continued. "Mike, you're supposed to be returning from your Hong Kong and Japan trip the Thursday before the party. So, I'm moving your flight so that you will arrive in L. A. on Wednesday, instead. You can go to Hollywood the next day and see if there's anything worthwhile. Then, instead of flying home, just head to Las Vegas Friday morning, I know you'll be jet-lagged, but you can manage." Mavis smiled and sat down breathless.

"*Don't be cruel,*" interjected Mike.

"Don't worry, honey. I'll be there with my *loving arms* to meet you," reassured Val. They all laughed.

Catching a second wind, Mavis continued, "The rest of us will make the sixteen hundred mile trek in the SUV. We'll leave on Monday. That will give us time to make a few stops, along the way, to hunt for anything Elvis-wise. Being in a car will also make it easier for Lisa and Marie. Cilla and Elvis can share the driving."

Everyone was silent as they all digested the plan and its ramifications.

"Well, *it's now or never*," said Mavis. "All in favor of the plan, say 'aye'." There was a chorus of ayes. "Those opposed?" asked Mavis. All was quiet.

The silence was broken by Cilla. "Say, aren't you all forgetting one very important thing? Since we're all there for the party on Friday, and it's our anniversary on Sunday, wouldn't it be a nice idea if we all renewed our vows on Saturday? Lisa and Marie could be part of the celebration. They could be like a *good luck charm*. You know what I mean? I can search the Internet and see if Kid Galahad is still around, and if he could come and perform the ceremony. He was so cool."

Everyone concurred it was a great idea, and left it to Cilla to make the arrangements.

She called Father Roades back to give him the good news that they would all be attending the party.

"Say Father, we would all like to renew our wedding vows on the Saturday. Do you know if the last booking that day is available? And I'll see if Kid Galahad is still around and can make it to perform at our ceremony. But instead of us renewing our vows to him singing them as we did the first time, I think, I would kind of like you to officiate. It would be nice to have a minister perform the ceremony this time." She immediately worried she might have spoken for herself, without considering the wishes of the others. She hoped they would agree with her snap decision.

"My dear, it would be my pleasure," he responded. "I'll check the schedule, and pencil you in. If there's an issue, I'll get back to you."

"Oh, good. Thank you, Father." Somehow she felt relieved and reassured. "We'll call and make reservations at the Bella Del Mundo. Are you aware if they have professional and vetted babysitters? My girls are just under five years old. I want to make sure there is someone trustworthy to look after them."

"I'll give you the phone number of Chad. He and his wife, Pru, own the Bella Del Mundo, and I'm sure you'll find him very helpful. Being a first class resort, I imagine all their staff and amenities are "top-of-the-line" as they say. Chad is overseeing the entire party. He and Pru were also married on the same day as the party and will obviously be attending."

"Sounds great. Good luck, Father, in tracking down the rest of the people. We're all looking forward to being there. I know I sure am."

"I'm looking forward to all of you being here, too. Goodbye, Cilla."

They hung up, and she started a Google search on her computer for Kid Galahad, Las Vegas. The phone rang.

"Elvis Online Memorabilia. Cilla speaking. How can I help you?" she answered.

Chapter 10
A Cruel Wheel of Fortune

Mattie placed her six-month-old baby, Garth Jr., in his crib for his regular afternoon nap. She pulled up the little, lemon-colored blanket to cover him and removed the pacifier from his mouth. Gently kissing him on his forehead, she smiled with pride and joy as her hand gently caressed his cheek.

Seating herself at the desk in the makeshift office of her small apartment, above the Harley repair shop, she started wading through the pile of bills. The past due notices, final demands, and threatening collection warnings were overwhelming her. *I know, I'll sort them into order. That way it will be easier to pay them. I can't believe I've been so terribly neglectful. My suppliers deserve better.* She heard the sound of a Harley entering the space below. As the engine was switched off, the muffled voices of the mechanics broke the silence. The sound of footsteps climbing the stairway was a sign that her solitude was about to be interrupted.

"Come in," she said in response to the knock at her door.

A greasy mechanic opened the door and stuck his head in. "I wanted to let you know that Ray's Harley is now ready for pick up. I replaced the brakes and test rode it. It will just be a standard materials charge and two hours labor. Dan asked me to tell you he is still a ways off from finishing his bike's service."

"Thanks, John. I'll call Ray and let him know as soon as I've generated the invoice."

"You all right, Mattie? You don't sound your normal self." John stepped inside the office and looked at her questioningly.

"Oh, I'm fine. Thanks, John. I was just thrown a bit of a curve earlier today."

"Anything I can help you with?"

Mattie shook her head before looking up at him. She bit her lip and took a deep breath. "I received a call from the clergyman at the chapel where Garth and I married almost five years ago. He invited us to a retirement party for one of the staff members in the New Year. I didn't know what to tell him. Can you believe that?"

John immediately felt uncomfortable and shifted from one foot to another while scratching his head, not knowing what to say.

"Of course, I had to tell him that we couldn't attend because of what happened to Garth. How a hit and run drunk ran a red light causing his accident."

"Gee, I'm sorry, Mattie. I know it must be really hard. We miss him down in the shop, too. Anything I can do for you?"

"I didn't mean to unload on you. I just need to call the minister back. He started asking some questions, and I just couldn't deal with them at the time. I'll be fine."

"You sure?"

Mattie nodded.

"Well, you just holler downstairs if you need us, you hear?" John was as sincere as he could be, and meant what he said, but was relieved to be able to retreat to the repair shop below. Mattie viewed the call received log on the telephone, looked for the Las Vegas area code, and dialed the number.

"I'm sorry, Father. I don't remember your name. This is Mattie Bridges calling from Harley Helper in Jackson, Mississippi."

"Ah, yes. This is Father Mark Roades. I'm so pleased you called back, and my condolences on your loss."

"Thank you, Father. I wanted to apologize for cutting you off like I did. It was only last month at Thanksgiving that Garth was killed. Your phone call brought back warm memories of my wedding day. As you can imagine, I'm still in a state of shock over losing my husband."

"I really am sorry, Mrs. Bridges. I hope family and friends have been supportive."

"To tell you the truth, Father, we don't have any family to speak of. Garth was raised in a number of foster homes and didn't get on well with any of his siblings or foster parents. I'm an only child. My mother died a few years back, and I don't speak to my father."

"Maybe now is the time to make amends. I'm sure he loves you."

"Father, the only person who ever truly loved me was Garth. We traveled across the southern states together on our Harleys five years ago. When we set out, it was never our intent to get married. But during the course of the journey, we fell in love. It was the most magical time of my life. We were so much in love and married at your aptly named Chapel of Eternal Love." She paused. "I don't know how I'm going to cope without him. We didn't have many friends.

Garth was a different soul. People couldn't warm up to him."
She grabbed a tissue from the box on her desk and clasped it
in her hand. She could feel the tears welling up in her eyes.
"But I could see all the goodness in his shielded heart. He
treated me like a queen, and I thought of him as my knight
in shining armor."

"I mentioned to you earlier about coming out for
Rosemary's retirement party. Maybe a change of scenery and a
return to the chapel will bring you some solace, some comfort?
Perhaps, the change might do you good?"

"That's out of the question, Father. I think that what you
are doing for that lady is very nice, but there's no way I can
make it now. I have a Harley repair shop to run, and it has
been on auto-pilot the last few weeks. I need to get the bills
paid and the business back on track. It is year-end coming up,
and I have all the tax filings and what-have-you to deal with.
Plus, I have a son to take care of."

"A son? Why, that's wonderful. How old is he?"

"It's not that wonderful, Father. Garth Jr. is only six
months old. He'll never know his daddy or the kind and loving
man he was." She covered her mouth as she felt herself starting
to cry aloud.

Mark could feel her pain. "I have a friend in a ministerial
position in Mississippi. Would you like me to have him call
you?"

"Oh, no, Father. I just need some time," she said between
the sobs. "But thank you all the same."

"Well, as the cliché goes, time is a great healer, and I do
believe that to be true."

Garth Jr. started to cry in his cot. "Excuse me, Father. My

baby is crying. I really need to go tend to him," she said, still fighting back the tears.

"I understand. But if you change your mind about coming out here for the retirement party, please call me. We'll send you an invitation, anyway. And by the way, should you ever need someone to talk to, or someone to listen, you have my telephone number."

"Thank you, Father. I appreciate it. Goodbye." She hung up, wiped her eyes, and ran to pick up Garth from his crib.

"I think it's time for a little diaper change, isn't it, my precious one?" she said carrying him into the bathroom. His crying subsided, and he fell quiet as she started to sing softly. He gurgled and kicked his legs happily while his mother diapered him and changed his clothes. Rocking Garth gently in her arms, holding him close to her heart so he could hear it beating, she placed a pacifier in his mouth and moved to the living room. She sat on the sofa, still holding him as she sang.

The voice of Father Roades suggesting a change of scenery might bring her some solace and comfort replayed over and over in her mind like a tired refrain of a song. His words, "perhaps the change might do you good," echoed constantly.

Never having lived anywhere outside of Mississippi, Mattie started to imagine what life in Las Vegas would be like. What was to keep her in Jackson? The business had been good and was very profitable. Yes, she was behind in the bills, but that was only because she'd been grieving. There was plenty of money to cover them all. Maybe she could sell the shop to her two mechanics, Dan and John.

No, I can't sell the business, she thought. *I would be betraying Garth. He built this company from scratch with his own bare hands. He loved it so much and was so proud of it. I just can't do it.*

Yet, a voice inside told her to take a chance. If she stayed where she was, she'd be haunted by ghosts from the past—waiting for Garth to join her on his lunch break, sporting his soiled red and white polka-dot bandana—expecting him to run up the stairs to give her a kiss on the cheek, hug her with his tattoo-filled arms and his outstretched greasy palms, and telling her how much he loved her.

She looked out the living room window and onto the street, watching the passersby, and felt very much alone. Her once secure and loving home and environment was now hollow and empty.

Garth Jr. had fallen asleep again, and she laid him back down in the crib. She looked at his chubby little face, which was already taking on a strong resemblance to hers, although he definitely had his father's eyes. With the baby snoozing, it was time for her to return to the desk, pull out the checkbook, and start getting those bills caught up.

But Mattie was unable to resist doing a computer search on Las Vegas apartments, and she became totally absorbed in the myriad of rentals that popped up on her screen. The sound of footsteps interrupted her as there was another knock at the door. This time it was Dan.

"Harley is ready for customer pickup, Ma'am. Here are the details of the repair." He handed her a sheet of paper with his hard to decipher scrawl.

Mattie suddenly realized she had not made the promised call, after John had come up earlier, saying Ray's motorcycle was ready. "I'll call your customer right away, Dan. Thank you."

She bolted back to reality. *I'm going to have to take a leaf out of Scarlett O'Hara's book on this one, and think about Las Vegas tomorrow. After all, tomorrow is another day,* she thought as she dialed Ray's number.

Chapter 11
Tender is the Night

Taylor was trimming the artificial Christmas tree, as he listened to one of his all time favorite movies, "Holiday Inn," on the television. His two little pug dogs were running around his feet, but he loved them too much to shoo them away, just as long as they didn't break one of his ornaments or, more importantly, one of the treasures belonging to Sherri. He always made sure there was an equal amount of ornaments from both their lives before they married.

"I *am* counting my blessings, Bing," he said aloud as Bing Crosby was crooning the famous song on the television. "My number one blessing is Sherri, and my number two and three blessings are my two little pooches, Lady and Tramp."

He broke from decorating and ventured round the wet bar into the open-plan kitchen to see how his lasagna dinner was coming along. Sherri would be home soon, and he thought he would surprise her with the tree trimmed and a nice, home-cooked meal. The table was all set. *So what if the candle is half-used? Better than to let it go to waste.*

As he finished placing the tinsel on the tree, he heard the sound of his old Ford pull up in front of the apartment building. *I'd recognize the sound of those screeching brakes a mile away. Really must take the car in and get it fixed. Wish we could get a newer second-hand car. Oh well, maybe next year.* It had always been his nature to live for the moment.

The dogs started yapping excitedly, sniffing at the front door, their stubby, little tails wagging back and forth. Taylor switched out the lights in the small living room to show off his lit Christmas tree to maximum effect. As he heard the sound of the front door knob turning, he hastily opened it.

"Oh my goodness," said Sherri, her voice full of excitement. "It's beautiful! It's magical!" She was ignoring the dogs jumping up and down, dying to be acknowledged by their mistress. Taylor gave her a big kiss on the cheek.

"Good to have you home, honey."

"And what's that delicious aroma? Have you made dinner? What's the occasion?"

"Never mind about me, how was your day?"

"Exhausting," she responded.

"Why don't you put your feet up, and let me pour you a drink?"

"Goodness. It *is* a special occasion, if we're having drinks." She was too tired to inquire further and taking her husband's advice, kicked off her shoes, stretched out on the couch, and put her feet up. Taylor returned with her wine, placed it on the nearby badly-stained, wooden coffee table, positioned himself at the other end of the couch, and started massaging her feet.

"What a godsend you are. That feels like sheer heaven. I did well at the coffee shop today. Ben's giving me the best tables now. I'm sure you'll count my tips later. People really are generous at this time of the year."

"Ben *should* give you the best tables. You've been there almost six years now. You're one of his most loyal employees."

"I should be loyal. I owe my livelihood to him for giving

me a job—and to you for being there that night when I called you at the suicide hotline center. Remember?"

"I remember," Taylor responded in a quiet voice. There was a momentary silence.

"My feet are killing me. Don't think I could work the streets, like I used to."

"I thought we weren't going to talk about that part of your life, anymore."

"Well, you can't ignore it. Let's face it, I was a hooker. It's a part of me."

Taylor ignored her comment. "I have some good news for you. I'll tell you at dinner which, by the way, has got to be ready by now."

Sherri watched her husband head toward the kitchen. *What in the world did I do to deserve this gem of a man? He gives me so much and wants so little in return. How I love him.* She listened to him whistling along to the tune, "White Christmas," as the movie was finishing on the television and watched him plate the salad and remove what smelled like delicious garlic bread from the oven.

"Sweetheart, dinner is served."

Sherri rose and headed to the beautifully set dining room table, as Taylor placed the plated lasagna, side salad, and bread on the table. He switched off the television and started to play a CD of holiday music. They clinked their merlot-filled glasses in a toast and savored the wine.

"So, what's this all about?" Sherri smiled, noticing her husband was wearing his boyish grin. She knew he had something to share.

"Well, this morning was my half-day at the animal shelter,

and they gave me my annual Christmas bonus. One hundred and fifty dollars. I know it's not a fortune, but for an animal shelter it's pretty good and means we can have a really nice Christmas. Maybe, we can even go to the movies or out to dinner one night."

"Why, that's wonderful. Congratulations!" Sherri beamed with joy. "Although, I don't know whether we can go out to dinner; what with you working at the suicide center and your volunteer duties reading to the sick at the hospital, and my juggling evening shifts at the coffee shop. You know, if it wasn't for Annie calling in sick today, and me having to go in, I wouldn't have been home this evening."

"I know. But occasionally it happens, like tonight. Look how wonderful it is with just the two of us. The unexpected is always full of joyous surprises."

The two of them continued to chat like newlyweds for the duration of their dinner. "Oh, I almost forgot," said Taylor, as he finished the last morsel of lasagna on his plate. "My second bit of exciting news. Remember the Chapel of Eternal Love where we got married?"

"Of course! How could I forget? The funny little dog that retrieved some biscuits from his bowl then dropped them in front of your feet. He had that doleful expression on his face."

Taylor laughed.

Sherri continued. "And how about that lovely lady who gave us both a big hug and said what a beautiful couple we made? We'd never even met her before. And you responded, 'I don't know about that'." She laughed as she mimicked him.

"And she said that beauty comes from within," Taylor recalled.

"She was so right about that." Sherri looked at him adoringly while reaching across the table to caress his cheek with her hand. He kissed and held it, enjoying the warmth and tenderness.

"It was the happiest day of my life," Taylor said.

"Mine too."

They gazed in each other's eyes savoring the moment of reminiscence. The dogs suddenly barked, causing them both to jump, signifying it was now their time for dinner and doggie treats.

Jolted back to the current time, Taylor rose and took the plates out to the kitchen. Sherri followed. He started to make the dinner for Lady and Tramp as he continued with his second piece of good news. "Today, I heard from the new pastor, Father Mark. He wasn't the one who married us. Anyway, it appears they're planning a surprise farewell party for that lady. Her name is Rosemary. She's retiring on the day of our fifth wedding anniversary, and they're trying to reunite all the couples who married on that day."

"What a sweet idea and such a nice gesture on behalf of the new pastor."

"Well, it wasn't exactly his idea. He said the concept came from a Pastor Glen, the man who originally built the chapel." Taylor laughed. "I also asked Father Mark if the little dog was still alive. His name is Buster. Apparently he is, but is getting old and moving much slower. I suppose we all are." He placed the dog bowls on the floor and washed his hands.

"Well, what did you say to him?"

"He just wanted our address to send the invite but said to make sure we RSVP'd. I told him we'd go, of course. I'm sure you can switch shifts with Annie if it's a night you are scheduled to work. I checked the calendar, and it's a day when I give my psychic readings, but I can forego those for one day."

He turned to face her, and taking her hands started to slow dance to the music playing. "It's that time of year when the world falls in love," he crooned to the orchestral version of "The Christmas Waltz" as they moved slowly.

My feet are so sore, but I can't disappoint him. "Where's the party going to be held?" she asked, trying to deflect the thoughts from her pain.

"It will be at that new luxury hotel and casino Bella Del Mundo. Apparently, the owners got married there the same day as we did. They'll be hosting."

Sherri looked mortified. "I can't go there. You *know* I can't go there."

Taylor was surprised. "Why ever not?"

"I don't belong there. I've nothing to wear. I'd be out of place."

Taylor was stunned. "What do you mean? You belong there as much as anyone else. We'll use my bonus to get you something to wear if that's the issue."

She stopped dancing and pushed his hands down. "Look at me, Taylor. I'm an aging hooker ... a common prostitute." As she moved away and sat on the couch, he followed sitting beside her, putting his arms around her. She looked at him with a worried, pained expression. There were tears in her eyes. "What you're looking at is a tired, aging tart, whose looks have faded, has graying hair and wrinkles, and who can't even afford to have a manicure regularly."

The music stopped as the CD finished and it was quiet.

The lights were twinkling on the Christmas tree. Even the dogs sensed the moment and curled on the floor.

Taylor lifted Sherri's chin and held her head in his hands. He remembered fondly the first time he'd gone to her home and she'd cooked the first home-made meal he had enjoyed in years. He kissed her on the forehead and remarked slowly and lovingly, "What I'm looking at is a beautiful soul."

She embraced his warmth as he held her tightly in his arms.

Chapter 12
Such a Beautiful World

"That's a wrap," said the producer, as the TV interview came to a close. He turned to the studio audience.

"Can we please have another round of applause for today's special guest, Miss Renee Kingsgate? Thank you for being with us today." He turned and gestured to the lady seated on the couch next to the interviewer. The audience applauded loudly. Smiling, Renee stood up and took a small bow while removing the microphone from the lapel of her dress.

"Thank you for having me on the show," she said in her demure, sultry voice.

The producer turned back to the audience. "Ladies and gentlemen, you can see this broadcast on your local network at six o'clock this evening, and thank you for attending today." He removed his headphones and stepped away from the set.

Renee returned to the dressing room and immediately called her husband. She was in New York promoting the addition of bath salts to their *Repent* line of beauty products.

Peter was buried in paperwork and emails, but recognizing her number on his cell phone, he immediately answered it. "Hi beautiful, how's it going?"

"Well, it's still freezing here in New York. The TV interview went extremely well, though. But I miss you, sweetheart. I hate it when you're not with me on these trips."

"I hate not being with you, too. Home is empty, and the nights are lonely. On the positive side, everywhere you've been, you've blazed a trail. Orders for the bath salts have been coming in by the boat loads from the department stores and beauty salons. They're following you."

"It's not the initial orders I worry about, it's a matter of whether there are follow-up orders. Those are the ones that count."

"You needn't bother your pretty little head over things like that. The launch of the hand and face cream last year did well, as did the launch of the eau de toilette and talcum powder the year before. We're on a roll."

"That's because I have the best marketing manager on the planet, and I adore you for it," she purred.

"And you're the most beautiful ambassador for our product, and I love you for that. But hey, guess what? I have some interesting news for you. I heard from the minister at the Chapel of Eternal Love, where we were married five years ago."

"Aha! You remembered our anniversary is coming up, or did the minister have to remind you?" Her voice was taunting and, to Peter's ears, was as seductive as always.

"What do you mean, did I remember our anniversary? How could I ever forget the most memorable day of my life when I married the most fantastic woman in the world?"

"And when I married the most loveable man," she laughed back.

"Furthermore, when have I ever forgotten our anniversary and not surprised you?" he boasted.

"I know. I was just kidding. But what was the call about?"

"Well, it appears that on our fifth anniversary, Rosemary, the lady in the office, is retiring. The night before, they're having a surprise farewell party at the Bella Del Mundo. They're trying to round up all the people who married that day five years ago."

"Fancy that. I wonder how a little wedding chapel can spring for a party there? It can't be cheap."

"Apparently, Pru and Chad Nelson, the owners of the resort were married at the chapel the same day we were. They were invited as guests and have offered to host it. They'll be sending the invitation."

"Oh yes, I remember reading about their marriage in the paper. She married a guy much younger than herself. He was reported to be a gigolo. Well, as long as they're happy that's all that matters, I suppose. Anyway, what did you tell the minister? Was he the same one who married us?"

"No, he's a new one who's been there about three years. He seems a nice, likeable fellow. I told him I'd speak to you. It looks like we have no trips planned at that time. I mentioned how Rosemary saved our wedding day; how we had planned it to be private and yet the media had found out and were at the chapel ready to pounce. Remember how she sensed what was happening and had the foresight to lock the chapel door, so our wedding ceremony could be private and sacred? I'll always be thankful to her for that."

"Me too," Renee responded softly, as she thought back to her wedding day. She suddenly started to chuckle. "Do you remember the little dog and how he barked so ferociously at the reporters through the office door? What a smart little pooch. We should have let him loose on that gaggle."

"Yes, that's right. I'd almost forgotten about the dog." Peter laughed, remembering the commotion.

"So, what have you been up to while I've been gone? I hope you've been a good boy."

"The best," he replied. "In fact, I've been formulating the idea for our next product. How about diversifying our line to include makeup? I was thinking we could market a whole line of lipsticks in different colors and shades. You could model them when they first come out, and I could kiss those pretty lips of yours to make sure there are no unsavory flavors coming from the different colors. I'll be the chief taste-tester."

"Now you're just being silly." She laughed. There was a knock at the dressing room door.

"Miss Kingsgate, our limousine is waiting to take you back to your hotel."

Renee placed her hand over the mouthpiece of the phone. "I'll be right out," she called to the anonymous voice. "I've got to go," she said, picking up her handbag. "The limo is waiting. I'll call you later. Looking forward to going to the party. Sounds like fun. Love you."

"Back at you, honey."

After they hung up, Peter waded through the myriad of emails that had come through on his computer since he'd last checked earlier that morning. There was one advising him of a potential strike at the European plant in Germany—another about a possible new distributor for their product line in South America—yet another from their media consultant about more advertising for the *Repent* bath salts. It was just a typical day in his world. He called the chapel.

"Hi Father. This is Peter Sharpstone from *Repent* calling you back."

The father thought for a moment. "*Repent*? Ah, yes, Peter," he stumbled. "I'm sorry. I thought your name was Kingsgate."

"No, that's my wife's maiden name."

"Forgive me, I'm sorry."

"No problem, Padre. People make that mistake all the time. It comes with having a famous wife." He laughed heartily. "I wanted to let you know that I've spoken to Renee. She and I would love to attend the party for Rosemary."

"That's great, Peter. I'll put you down for two. You needn't RSVP to the invite when you get it, I'll let the Nelsons know you're coming."

"I'm curious about one thing though, Father. If the last day for Rosemary is on the 19th, why is the party being held on the 18th? No big deal. I'm just curious."

"Rosemary and I have been invited to some friends of hers on the last day, so that's why we made it the night before."

"Makes sense. By the way, do you have a photographer for the event?"

"I hadn't even thought about that. Why? Do you know a good one?"

"How about me? I was a photographer before I married Renee. That was my business, and I still take all the *Repent* shots of my wife. Typically, I don't do any other now because handling the business and photographing Renee is pretty much a full time job."

"I didn't know you were responsible for that wonderful photography. Of course, I'm familiar with the product line

Repent. I think we all know those commercials. Naturally, they appeal to me because of the brand name," Mark joked.

Peter laughed back. "Yes, I can see that. So, how about I take some nice shots of the party, and I can get it into an album for Rosemary before she finishes her last appointment on Saturday? Beforehand, I'll get some nice ones of the chapel—discretely of course—some of the Bella Del Mundo, and take a slew of pictures of all the guests at the party. It will be a nice little souvenir gift for her."

"What a very generous gesture, but I certainly wouldn't want to put you to all that trouble."

"It's no trouble at all, Father. It will be our pleasure. As I mentioned to you, Rosemary saved our wedding from the pack of wolves who had no respect for our privacy that day." There was a beep on his cell phone. He recognized the phone number on his display pad as Renee. "Anyway, Father, must go. Have to take another call. Please, let us know if you need anything else." He hurriedly disconnected and answered, "Where are you, honey?"

"Lying down in the hotel room, wishing you were here with me. I guess there'll be no lipsticks in our immediate future."

"Oh? Why not?"

"Because, my precious one. I've just heard from my gynecologist." She started to cry with happiness. "There's going to be an addition to our family. You and I are going to be proud parents."

"Yippee!" Peter shouted as he leapt from his chair and starting jumping up and down. He saw the puzzled faces of the staff in the warehouse below looking up at him through his glass window. He quickly opened the door and yelled to them, "I'm going to have a baby!" He slammed the door shut again.

Tears of joy continued running down Renee's face. "Oh, Peter. I can't believe it, after all this time. I'm so excited. I hope I make a good mother." She started to babble.

"You'll be the best mother, because you've been the best wife. If the baby is a girl, she'll be as beautiful as you are."

"And if the baby is a boy, he'll be as smart and charming as his father."

"Honey, I'm booking the next available flight out of here to join you in New York. I just need to be with you. I love you *so* much, Renee. I'm calling the airline now."

"See you soon. Fly safely."

Peter didn't even go home to grab an overnight bag or change of clothing. *I can buy all the necessities when I get there,* he reasoned. He climbed into his Jaguar, called the airline from his car phone, and drove hastily to the airport.

Chapter 13
Defying the Odds

Sally pulled into the parking lot of her daughter's apartment building and looked forlornly at the drab, stucco complex. *I wish they could have found somewhere on the ground floor or at least a building with an elevator,* she thought as she climbed the two flights of stairs to the unit on the top floor.

"Mama," said Betty-Sue as she opened the front door. "This is a surprise. I wasn't expecting you. Sorry, I've just put little Rosemary down for her afternoon nap." She gave her mother a hug and kiss on the cheek. "Would you like some coffee?"

"Sure, I'll take a cup. Can I just go and take a quick peek at my granddaughter?"

"As long as you promise not to wake her." Betty-Sue busied herself in the kitchen loading the dishwasher and wiping the sink.

Her mother stepped inside the very small nursery. The walls had been painted a pastel pink since she last visited. A collection of cardboard characters from *Winnie the Pooh* hung from the ceiling and were twirling as a result of the soft, gentle breeze blowing from the fan, turning slowly back and forth, on the little wooden dresser. An assortment of cuddly teddy bears and other fluffy animals cluttered the corner table. Sally peeked inside the crib and observed her granddaughter sleeping peacefully. *Rosie looks so like my precious Betty-Sue when she was her age,* she thought, smiling lovingly down at the baby. Since Betty-Sue was not there, she quietly opened the dresser drawers to see what was inside and was relieved to find an assortment of bibs, diapers, knitted booties, and other baby garments all neatly folded and organized.

Satisfied, Sally left the little room and returned to the sparsely-furnished living room to see if there were any new additions or improvements. There was a small Christmas tree in the corner, adorned with an abundance of "Baby's First Christmas" ornaments. She admired Betty-Sue and Derek, her son-in-law, who were making it on their own, even if she didn't approve of the way they were handling things.

"I just love your new throw pillows. But how can you afford them?" Sally asked pointedly, sitting herself on the couch. She picked up one of silk, ruffled pillows and immediately looked for the designer label.

Betty-Sue loved her mother, but was often irked by her interference and insinuations.

"If you must know, Mama, Melanie let me have them at a huge discount. One of her clients had purchased them as part of her interior-designing package and then rejected them." Still in the kitchen, Betty-Sue removed the soiled filter from the coffee pot and glared at her mother across the counter that separated the rooms.

"Melanie sure treats you well, considering you're just a part-time employee."

"My boss thinks I have promise as an interior designer, Mama. She believes in me."

"I do too, sweetie. I know you'll get your degree someday."

Betty-Sue raised her eyebrows. "Mama, both Derek and I are doing really great. He's learning a lot working for the architect friend of his. By studying at the University of Phoenix, I'll be getting my degree in interior design, just as I always dreamed."

"Eventually, I suppose. But, it's not a *real* degree," her mother argued. "I mean, it's an online computer school for goodness sake. It's not like getting a degree at Wellesley." She threw up her hands.

"I would never have gone to Wellesley, Mama. We both know that. Besides, the degree I'm getting is as good as any. I'm able to study during the day while I watch Rosemary. After Derek gets home, I go with Melanie for a couple of hours when she meets clients at their homes and discusses wallpaper, couches, artwork, and everything. I'm learning so much from her. While I'm gone, Derek does his studying at the University of Phoenix and watches Rosemary. Derek's folks help out from time to time, which is great. We manage."

"What's that supposed to mean?" asked her mother in an icy tone.

Betty-Sue brought her mother's coffee into the living room and handed her the mug. She sat down in the large blue, oversized bean-bag chair which was next to the end of the couch where Sally was sitting and stared at her mother.

"Nothing, Mama. It means nothing. I'm just telling you the facts. It's not easy, but we all know dad hasn't spoken to me since the day Derek and I left Las Vegas. I don't know if he'll ever get over the fact that we ran off to get married and that I was pregnant. Even though we didn't get married that day, he never came to our wedding later here in Pomona or to

Rosemary's christening. He resents Derek and it's caused a rift between the two of you and Derek's folks."

Betty-Sue reached out and placed her hand over her mother's. "I'm sorry for all that. But it's behind us. I can't put the spilled milk back in the bottle."

Sally patted her daughter's hand and held on. She looked into Betty-Sue's eyes.

"Your father is a stubborn man, sweetie and always has been. Not only that, he feels guilty that you miscarried. He thought you probably were under a lot of stress, and he feels he added to it. Until that point, he was slowly beginning to soften."

"I don't blame dad for my miscarriage. It just happened. A lot of factors probably contributed. Fortunately, God's given us Rosemary, the jewel of my life. I really am very happy, Mama."

"I can see that. And I can see what a wonderful mother you are. But, of course, you would be. Little Rosie was born on Mother's Day."

Betty-Sue smiled. "Her name is Rosemary, not Rosie," she chided.

"Of course, I know how you hate it when I call her Rosie. I can't help it. She looks like a little Rosie. But I almost forgot. It's about Rosemary that I came to visit. Not our Rosemary, but the Rosemary from that wedding chapel in Las Vegas who you named your daughter after."

"*That* Rosemary? What? She called?"

"Actually, she didn't. It was the minister who called me. Apparently, when you and Derek filled out the forms you didn't list any phone contact information. He found a phone number scribbled on the side of the forms and called it. It was our phone number. It must be from when Rosemary called us that day, telling your dad you were pregnant and how special it would be for him to become a grandfather. Anyway, she is retiring on the date you went there to get married. They're holding a surprise farewell party and inviting back all the couples who were married on that day five years ago."

"But Derek and I didn't get married."

"Well, the minister doesn't know that. He's just going through the records."

Betty-Sue became wistful as she recalled the day she and Derek arrived at the chapel. How frightened she'd been and how uncertain their future looked. Such a comfort Rosemary's kind words and help had meant to her. Sally sensed what her daughter was thinking and removed her hand from her daughter's and caressed her cheek. *How my little girl has matured from that day.* She regretted that Betty-Sue had not enjoyed her final teenage years, but was proud of how she had grown into adulthood.

"Did you tell the minister we named our baby after Rosemary?"

Her mother nodded.

Betty-Sue continued, shaking her head. "Thinking back, I don't know how I could have gotten through that day had it not been for her. She was so calm and reassuring. All the while, that little dog of hers was gnawing and gnashing on his bones and toys in the office. Too bad Rosemary's words to dad fell on deaf ears."

Sally ignored the comment. There was nothing more she could say or do. She was torn between her husband and daughter and had shed more than enough tears over the years about the situation. Opening her purse, she retrieved the phone number for the chapel. "Here's the minister's number. It's his direct phone line. I told him you would call. He asked for your address, so he could send you an invite, but I didn't give it to him. As I mentioned, it's a surprise party, and it's going to be held at that posh new Bella Del Mundo resort and casino. They're giving the rooms at highly reduced rates." She wanted to give her daughter some cash, but thought better of it, knowing how stubborn and independent both Betty-Sue and Derek were.

"Wow! That's awesome. It would be cool to go and take the baby to meet her namesake. We did send Rosemary a picture of her when she was born and told her we honored our promise. Maybe, Derek's parents could come along and babysit while we go to the party."

Sally was heartbroken. *Well, there will be no family events for me, as long as her father is in his stubborn frame of mind.* She was only too aware of all she was missing out on and struggled to fight back the tears. "Sweetie, I must run. I'm sure you need to get back to your studies, and I have a lot of errands to do before your father gets home. Let me stop in before I leave and blow a little kiss to Rosie—I mean Rosemary," she corrected herself and disappeared into the nursery.

Betty-Sue took her mother's cup into the kitchen, and the two met at the front door.

"Thanks for stopping by, Mama. I love you."

"I love you too, sweetie. Give Derek a hug for me."

They kissed and Sally left. Betty-Sue listened for a while to the sound of her mother's high-heeled shoes clicking intermittently as she descended the stairway. When the sound became distant, she closed the front door and went to check on her baby. Betty-Sue looked at the tiny little fingers sticking out from the pink onesie with its small, ruffled collar and marveled at the miracle, as she always did. Seeing her baby was safe, she returned to the living room and called Father Mark. She thought that before discussing it with Derek, it might be appropriate to see if they would still be invited under the circumstances.

"This is Betty-Sue calling from Pomona. I believe you spoke to my mother, Sally Pearson, earlier today?"

"Ah, yes. Indeed, I did. Did your mother tell you why I was calling?"

"Yes, she did. But I don't know if she told you that my husband and I weren't actually married that day."

"No, as a matter of fact, she didn't." He was not sure as to whether to pursue the line of conversation or not. "But she did tell me that you named your daughter after Rosemary. I'm sure Rosemary would be thrilled to know that."

"Oh, she knows. We promised her our baby would be named after her the day we were at the chapel. When the baby was born, we wrote to Rosemary and sent her a photo. She actually took the time out of her schedule and replied. She really is one of God's angels. That was certainly the case on our wedding day—or what would have been our wedding day."

"I don't understand," replied Mark, somewhat mystified.

"Of course not. Why would you? Derek and I come from homes with old-fashioned values. We're both from Oklahoma originally. Derek and I were childhood sweethearts. When I became pregnant, knowing how our parents would feel, we eloped. We were going to get married in Las Vegas and then head on to Reno or Idaho to look for a job. Of course, we were five years younger, and five years stupider, I guess. Rosemary sensed our anguish and how frightened we were, and not ready to make it by ourselves. She called our parents and managed to heal the breach … well for the most part. Derek's folks are fine now, as is my mother. But my Dad hasn't spoken to me since."

"Sorry to hear that. Must be hard for you."

"I've learned to live with it."

Mark decided to switch gears. "So, your little girl is five now?"

"No. Unfortunately, I miscarried. Derek and I waited three years and then got married. My daughter was born on Mother's Day this year."

"Well, I don't think that is sufficient reason for you not to attend Rosemary's party. After all, you were part of that day. Will you be able to come?"

Betty-Sue was relieved. "I haven't spoken to my husband yet. I wanted to see first whether we'd still be welcome. Then, we would need to see if it is in the budget."

"Didn't your mother explain to you, the rooms would be discounted?"

"Yes, she did. Even so, we still have to come up with the money."

"Well, I hope you can find a way to make it. I'm sure Rosemary would love to see you—and the baby. We'll be sending you an invite. Just RSVP when you know."

"I will, Father Roades, and thank you."

They hung up. Knowing how Derek disliked calls at work, she sat down, and waited patiently for him to come home. She hoped they could find a way to go to Rosemary's party.

Chapter 14

A New Life for Rosa

Pru and Chad were sitting behind the desks in their office. Pru was reading the mail which always came directly to her. Chad was studying the previous day's income reports.

"Well, honey. We've received our first complaint about the hotel," she said smothering her cigarette in a Limoges ashtray. "It's about Rosa of all people. I need to go downstairs to the convention center and greet all the bigwigs. Could you please deal with this?" She held a piece of paper in the air.

Chad rose and took the letter from her hand. "I find that hard to believe. We've never had a complaint about Rosa in the almost five years she's worked for us." He sat on the corner of her desk.

"I know. It's not as if the complaint is from some disgruntled tourist, either. The complaint is from our own Las Vegas resident, Judge Al Baines."

"Judge Baines? The well-known attorney that was always in the news—always involved in labor disputes? Is that the one?"

"Yes, the same. Apparently, he brought his wife here for a weekend to celebrate their Silver Wedding Anniversary and was dissatisfied with the room service Rosa provided. I'm assuming he wants us to fire her."

"Well, that's a bit extreme. As a labor attorney, he should know it's just not that simple to fire somebody."

"I'm not sure exactly what he wants. You know legal-speak. It is all written in such mumbo-jumbo, you never know what lawyers mean." She rose to leave. "I love you, honey," she said, kissing him and placing her hand on his other cheek.

He quickly took her hand and kissed it, while looking into her eyes. "Love you, too. Don't be too long with your bigwigs downstairs. Oh, and on your way out, could you ask Janice to track Rosa down and have her report to me in our office?"

"I will, and I'll be back as soon as I can. Be kind to Rosa. She's been a loyal and hardworking employee. I can't imagine what she's done that caused a judge to expend such valuable time complaining about her. I would have thought he had more important things on his mind."

Pru left and Chad returned to his desk to read the entire letter from Al Baines. Soon, there was a knock at the door. "Come in," he called out, looking up to see who it was. The door opened and Rosa entered. She was neatly dressed in her ivory uniform, her dark hair rolled in a bun.

"You wanted to see me, Señor Nelson?" she asked nervously, standing as close to the door as possible.

"Hello, Rosa. Yes, please come in and take a seat," he said, indicating the chair on the other side of his desk.

Rosa accepted his offer but eyed him suspiciously. The only time she was ever in their office was to deliver lunches as part of her job.

"How was it we came to hire you, Rosa?" he asked.

"It was through Señora Nelson. She good friends with Señora Rosemary from wedding chapel," Rosa responded in her broken English.

"Did you get married at that chapel?"

"*Sí*. Well, no. I was already married. I had husband and four boys in Guatemala. I come here for work because my husband, he need money for eye surgery. I need a work permit to get job. Señora Nelson, she help me to get work permit."

"Yes, I remember that. So, what was your connection to the wedding chapel?"

"I think, only way for me to get work permit is to marry American. I do what I must because I love my husband and four sons. But Jake, he American who I come to chapel to marry, he steals my money and leaves me at chapel. I have nothing and no one."

"So you were prepared to commit bigamy?"

"Please? I no understand."

"Never mind. It's not important. Where are your husband and sons living now?"

"They here in America with me. I make good money with tips. My husband have his surgery. There is group here called "Friends of Guatemalans". They help with money for operation and our church, it help too. Now, my husband he work. He taxi driver. We very happy and life is good for us. Boys learn how to play baseball. They all speak good English now. They all at school."

Chad looked at the beautiful young lady sitting across from him. *Too bad your English hasn't improved*, he thought. He appreciated the determined and defiant, yet tender, look on her face. Clearly, she'd do anything for the husband and family she obviously loved so much. *She's like a proud lioness protecting her cubs. I can see she's been through quite an ordeal.*

"Do you know a gentleman called Al Baines?" he asked, looking directly at her.

Rosa thought for a moment before answering and lowered her eyes so she did not have to look at him. "*Sí,*" she said. "I know Señor Baines." She fell silent.

Chad leaned forward. "Do you care to elaborate?" Seeing the confused look on her face, he rephrased his question, "Sorry, can you tell me how you know him? Where did you meet?"

"Señor Baines, he not nice man. I work for him and his wife, Señora Elizabeth. Night before I have to go to chapel for marriage, Jake, who say he marry me and get me work permit, he want five hundred more dollars. I no have money. I go see Señora Elizabeth. She very nice lady and good to me. Maybe she lend me the money. She not home, and Señor Baines, he very drunk. He want sex from me for money. He flashes money on table. I so desperate, I start to take off my clothes for him, and he goes to make drink. I grab money from wallet he leave on table, and I run."

"You stole from him?"

Rosa looked downward again. She nodded. "I also take clock from shelf. I sell the clock and my wedding ring to get money. I told you. Jake, he take my money at the chapel and leave me there. I had nothing."

Chad looked intently at Rosa. "Does my wife know about any of this?"

"*Sí.* I tell Señora Nelson and Señora Rosemary everything. I do what I need to. It was no easy for me when I come to America. Señora Rosemary, she very kind to me. But only when Señora Nelson hire me and help me, then I know it be good in America.

Just like Pru to entangle herself in a sob story like this one.

Chad smiled in admiration of his wife. It was so typical of her to lend a helping hand. *I'm surprised she didn't pay for the eye surgery,* he thought. *For all I know, she probably did.* He picked up the letter from his desk and re-read part of it. "Mr. Baines has written a letter of complaint about you. He says you spilled the tray of food all over him. He says you were very careless. Is that true?"

"*Si.* He call for room service. I take him food and leave tray on table by window. He is laying in bed. He recognize me, and say his wife is in spa having massage. He ask me to bring tray closer to him and he sits up. I take tray to him, and he grab me. He hurt me, and I tell him to let me go. He no stop and shake me." She gestured with her hands to illustrate her point. "I tip tray of food over him. He deserve it. I no sorry for what I do. It is only way I can get him to stop."

Chad noticed the pain in her face as she relived the experience. "Rosa, you know the rules. If any guest approaches or touches you inappropriately, you are to report it immediately. Why didn't you do that?" His tone was more one of concern than a stern admonition.

"I afraid he have me arrested for stealing from him if I report him. Is his word against mine. He a judge. I have no proof he grab me in hotel room."

A tear started to roll down her cheek. Chad rose from his chair and went to retrieve a box of tissues from Pru's desk drawer. He placed the box on his desk in front of Rosa. She quickly took one from the box and dried her eyes.

"You would have had marks, Rosa, which we would have seen and been able to confirm. He's not going to report you for stealing. As you said, he *is* a judge and obviously does not want the negative publicity and possible sexual harassment charges."

"I no understand."

Chad sighed. "Just consider yourself warned, Rosa. If it ever happens again with any guest, you are to report it immediately. Do I make myself clear? I do hope you understand, we have these rules for *your* protection. "

She nodded.

"Judge Baines has written this letter of complaint, and I'll deal with it. Now, you can return to your regular duties."

"Thank you, Señor Nelson." She rose and headed toward the doorway, then turned. "You no fire me?" she asked.

He shook his head. "No, Rosa, of course we're not firing you. As I said, consider yourself warned. You've been a loyal and hard working employee. You're part of our large family. We want you to feel happy and safe with us." He gave her a weak smile.

She smiled back, as she wiped another tear from her eye and turned again to leave.

"Oh, by the way, Rosa, did my wife speak to you about the farewell party for Rosemary, the lady at the wedding chapel?"

"*Si*, Mr. Nelson." Rosa beamed. "I make her nice scarf from Guatemalan wool as gift. Is almost finish. I hear is very cold in Carson City."

Chad smiled at the seemingly refreshing innocence of one who had endured so much. "Yes, is very cold in Reno," he emulated. "Are you able to switch your shift so you can attend?"

"*Si.*"

"Will you be bringing your husband … your real husband?"

Rosa's eyes lit up. "Can I bring him?"

"Well, of course you can. I'm surprised my wife didn't mention that."

"Thank you, Señor Nelson. Thank you and *Feliz Navidad*."

"And *Feliz Navidad* to you, Rosa," he replied as she left. He shook his head and picked up the letter from Judge Baines, wondering how he was going to respond.

I'll probably have to discuss with Human Resources, he thought. *Oh, I'll deal with this later. I wonder how Pru is getting on with those dignitaries. Maybe, I'll just go downstairs and see.*

He got up from his desk and headed for the door, stopping to twirl the ballerina on top of the music box. He whistled along to Chopin's *Nocturne* as he made his way toward the elevator.

Chapter 15

Love on the Rocks

"You work wonders with those hands, Diana. I always feel better after I've received one of your body massages. My sleep even improves. I wish I had the time to come every week." The middle aged lady slipped a twenty-dollar bill into the masseuse's hand.

Diana smiled. "Thank you. You *should* make the time to come every week. You owe it to your body. But I know you won't," she chided her client. "I'll look forward to seeing you next month. Hope you have a Happy Holiday and Happy New Year's," she said as her client left the salon.

"Diana, I didn't think that appointment would ever finish," Maxine, the young receptionist, gushed. "Look what came for you about half an hour ago. Who's the secret admirer? Oh, and by the way, your five o'clock just cancelled."

Diana turned and saw a large arrangement of red roses on the counter. Seeing her name on the card, she opened it.

"To my darling wife. Can we please have dinner this evening at our favorite restaurant? Have made reservations for 6:30— Your ever-loving husband, Mitch."

Diana was stunned.

"So who's the admirer? Come on, tell us all," teased Maxine.

Oblivious to the remark, Diana picked up the vase and headed toward her room.

"Say, are you all right, honey?" Maxine called.

Diana turned around. She was still shocked. "I'm sorry Maxine. Did you say something?"

"I just wondered if you were all right. You look as if you've seen a ghost."

"Oh. No. I'm fine. Thanks." Still in a daze, Diana continued down the corridor and into her room, closing the door behind her. She placed the flowers on the table and thought for a while. The sound of the rippling water, designed to help clear the mind, along with the piped-in music was soft and soothing.

What in the world is he up to? It's only a few months until the divorce becomes final. I've spent months preparing myself for this, coming to grips. What's he trying to do? Ah, who are you kidding, Diana? You know you still love the guy. Yeah, but who wants to stay married to an alcoholic?

Her tormented mind continued in circles as the dueling voices she heard raised questions and dredged up issues from the past. She looked at her watch and saw there was only ten minutes until her next appointment. Grabbing her cell phone from her uniform pocket, she dialed her husband. "What's all this about? Flowers? Dinner? Have you forgotten we're getting a divorce?"

He ignored her curt comments. "Did you like the flowers?"

She looked at the vase and the crimson rose buds peeking out through the baby's breath and greenery. They were twelve of the most perfectly-shaped stems she had ever seen. "They're absolutely beautiful. But what prompted them?"

"Can we discuss that over dinner at our favorite restaurant tonight?" He paused. There was no answer. "I've made reservations for two," he tempted.

Return to the Chapel of Eternal Love

Diana weighed the proposition in her mind. She had to admit, she was curious.

"Well, my last appointment of the day just cancelled. I suppose I'd have enough time to get home and change. But I won't have time to get my hair done."

"You always look beautiful, no matter how your hair looks."

Here he goes, exhibiting that same charm I fell in love with all those years ago. Her eyes became a little misty. "I have to go. My next appointment will be here any moment. I'll be home just after five."

It was hard for her to focus on her massages with the rest of her clients that day, but saying goodbye to her last customer came soon enough. She grabbed her purse and headed out the door.

"Hey, haven't you forgotten your flowers?" asked Maxine.

Diana smiled. "No. I think I'll leave them here, and my customers can enjoy them with me."

As she drove home, she thought her circumstances would probably appear odd to most people. After all, how many couples go through divorces and are still sharing the home together, if not the bed? *That's one thing I am going to have to deal with in the new year. Look for a new home after the divorce becomes final.* She had already decided just to rent, to give her time to ponder her future. *At least ours will not be an acrimonious divorce. I really am thankful for that. I do hope Mitch keeps his word, and we can still be friends.*

She pulled into the garage, and noticed the trash bins piled high. There was a smell of alcohol surrounding them. She wondered what state Mitch would be in, when suddenly he opened the door leading from the garage to the kitchen and smiled at her. *How dapper and handsome he looks,* she thought. *But then, whenever he was dressed up, he always did look like a fashion model.* She was relieved he was sober.

"What in the world … ?" Diana looked around the kitchen and into the open-plan living room. Everything was spotless. Her home was never dirty, but Mitch could be messy and leave things scattered. "Well, I can see how you spent your day off work today," she commented, noticing no plates in the kitchen sink, the newspaper neatly placed on the magazine rack beneath the coffee table, all the kitchen counters clean and, miracle of miracles, no beer bottles lying around.

She reached into the refrigerator for a bottle of water, and was surprised to see how everything had been rearranged so neatly. *What happened to all those bottles of beer? He couldn't possible have drunk them. He'd be out cold by now if he had.* Now, more confused than ever, she couldn't wait for dinner to find out what he was up to and hurried upstairs to shower and change.

"What happened to the flowers?" Mitch called after her.

"I thought I'd keep them at work. That way, my clients and I can enjoy them," she shouted back from the top of the stairs.

The conversation was stilted on the way to the restaurant. They exchanged pleasantries, and she thanked him for tidying the home, while hoping for a clue as to what was on his mind. But he was waiting until they were firmly seated at the restaurant before discussing his game plan.

"Welcome to Alize's," announced the maître d' as he escorted the couple to their reserved seating by the window, overlooking the Las Vegas Strip. Mitch was pleased their location was relatively secluded, and the tables on either side were empty. No sooner were they seated, when the wine steward stopped by to ask them their choice for cocktails.

"I'll take a Shirley Temple, thank you," said Diana. To her surprise, Mitch ordered a Diet Coke and declined to look at the wine menu. *Something is definitely afoot.* As soon as they were alone, Mitch started.

"I'm sure you're wondering what this is all about." He reached out for her hand. "Diana, I want us to give our marriage another try."

Immediately, she drew back in her chair and raised her hands. "Mitch, we've been through this a hundred times, and the answer is no."

"Just hear me out. Please," he begged.

She looked at him suspiciously, wondering what had instigated this new revelation. Not wishing there to be a scene in the restaurant, she held her tongue. "I'm listening."

"Today, I had a life-altering experience. The minister from that chapel where we married five years ago called. The lady who ran the show, remember the one with the little dog?" Diana nodded as Mitch continued, "She's retiring, and they're having some kind of surprise farewell party for her. The minister is trying to get everyone back who married that day. It's being held at Bella Del Mundo."

Diana was truly baffled. "And this relates to us, how?"

"His call was like a thunderbolt. I got to thinking about our wedding day. It made me think of our first wedding in California and how much in love we were. Yeah, I know I messed up big time by sleeping with Margot which led to our first divorce. But fate drew us back together here in Las Vegas, and I was so happy the day we married at that little chapel—the Chapel of Eternal Love. It was blissful. Just the two of us. All those wonderful memories we made. Now, here we are almost five years later, divorcing again. Where did we go wrong?"

Diana was not given the opportunity to respond as the drinks arrived, accompanied by a basket containing an assortment of breads and a myriad of flavored butters.

"May I take your orders, sir?"

Even though they had not looked at the menus, Mitch was sure what Diana would like. "Chateaubriand and lobster bisque?" he enquired of Diana. She nodded. "We'll both have the Chateaubriand—medium, please and lobster bisque."

"Very well, sir. Thank you." He removed the menus and departed.

Mitch noticed the expression on his wife's face, and corrected himself. "Okay, where did *I* go wrong is probably more accurate. But, you haven't forgiven me for the episode with Margot, even though I've been faithful ever since."

Diana leaned forward. "You don't get it, do you? I've forgiven you, even though Margot was my best friend and the wife of *your* best friend. I forgave you before we even married the second time. I resigned myself to that slice of history a long time ago. You're the one who hasn't come to terms with it. You can't deal with the guilt. That's why you drink so much. It's your drinking I can't handle. Never knowing whether I'm coming home to find you in a drunken stupor or not. After we married, you stopped going to your AA meetings and to the counseling sessions. The problem is, you're an alcoholic who is doing nothing about it. That's what I can't forgive."

"You're right. I know it. But I never discovered any benefits to the counseling. They may help some people, but the counselors didn't help me, neither did AA. Yet, today I started talking to that minister. His name is Mark Roades. I told him I didn't think we'd be attending the party. It hardly seems appropriate since we're going through a divorce. I told him that. We got to chatting and I spoke for half an hour. I felt bad as I took him away from his work, but somehow, we connected. He says he'd be happy to counsel me on a weekly basis. Also said, you could come, too, if you want. My first appointment is next week."

Diana was dubious. "What about AA?"

"Well, in case you didn't notice, I'm drinking Diet Coke."

Diana smiled and softened. "Yes, that didn't go unnoticed."

"Today, after I spoke to Father Roades, I opened all the bottles of beer in the house and emptied them in the sink. I did the same with the bottles of scotch and vodka."

"So, that was the odor of alcohol I smelled in the garage, was it? The empty bottles?"

"I mean it, Diana. I'm deadly serious about this. I love you so much. I always have, and I always will. Please, give me … give us … just one more chance."

"I don't know. It's a lot to absorb. It sure is a lot to ask."

"Well, will you at least come with me to meet the minister next week? And can I let him know we'll attend the party for that lady?"

"Her name was Rosemary, Mitch. I remember her. She was very sweet." *Mitch never did have a good memory for names.* "I'll think about it," she said.

"Can't you do better than that, honey?" he pleaded. "Come on, it's the season of goodwill."

The waiter arrived with their soup bowls and poured the lobster bisque.

"May I get you something else to drink? A glass of house wine, perhaps?"

"Just another Shirley Temple for the lady and another Diet Coke for me, please."

"Thank you, sir. Bon appétit."

Diana looked askance at her husband, as she picked up her soup spoon. *This is going to require some serious consideration,* she thought.

"I know it's a lot to lay on you, but can't you just give us one more try?"

"I said, I'll think about it. That's the best I can do," she replied. "Can we now just enjoy our dinner?"

Her heart was already beginning to soften as she looked at the boyish, dejected look on her husband's face.

Chapter 16

America the Beautiful

"Greetings to you, Father, and Merry Christmas," Phil said when he realized it was Mark Roades calling. "I hope you're not calling to cancel coming to the farewell dinner my wife and I are hosting for Rosemary after her last day."

"No, not at all. I'm looking forward to it. But I do happen to be calling about Rosemary. I ..."

Phil interrupted him. "Actually, Father, you've called at a pretty bad time. I'm expecting a houseful of guests for a party any moment now. As a matter of fact, Rosemary is coming after work. She's one of the invited guests. You're more than welcome to join us, too."

"Why, that's mighty kind of you. What's the occasion?"

"Oh, my wife's from Vietnam. Today, she became a United States citizen, and we've just returned from the swearing-in ceremony. It's a big day for her. She's so excited and so proud. We're having a celebration party."

"That *is* special. Absolutely, I'll stop by for a short while and give my congratulations. I have your address from your invite to the farewell dinner, so I know where you live. I'll discuss what I was calling you about when I see you."

As soon as they hung up, Phil turned around and saw Linh high on a ladder.

"Linh, be careful," he yelled to his daughter. "We don't want you falling."

"Stop fussing, Dad," she replied, pinning the red, white, and blue bunting into a corner of the drapery's valance, completing the loop around the room. "I'm not a kid anymore." She stepped down from the ladder and hugged her father.

"I know," said Phil. "I just wish I'd been there for you when you *were* a kid. To see you grow up." They both looked around the room and admired their decorations. Apart from the bunting draped from the ceiling around the room, "Old Glory" was a dominant presence in the corner. Cardboard replicas of the Statue of Liberty, the Lincoln Memorial, the White House, the Washington Monument, and Mount Rushmore all adorned the mantel and the end tables. Small red, white, and blue foil stars were scattered across the main coffee table. A stack of drink napkins sporting the words "God Bless America" were placed strategically on both ends of the wet bar.

Father and daughter walked into the kitchen to look at the buffet spread they'd prepared for their guests. It was simple Americana, more like a Fourth of July picnic, but it was what the guest of honor wanted and what she enjoyed most. A big bowl of potato salad alongside a colorful dish of fruit salad was positioned at one end of the table. A large platter of fried chicken occupied the center with room for the hot dogs behind. Linh lifted the lid of the large saucepan to check on the corn on the cob and began extracting them with the tongs. She placed them in a bowl at the end of the table alongside the rolls, hot dog buns, condiments, and the platter of deviled eggs. At a nearby table, patriotic-colored plastic knives and forks were spread next to the alternating red, white, and blue paper plates with matching napkins.

"Dad, why don't you go and see what's happened to mother? She should be here to greet the guests."

At that moment, Kim-Ly appeared in the doorway. "I *am* here. How do I look?" she asked, striking a pose. "Is it a little too much for the occasion?" Her diction was almost perfect, and Phil marveled at how adroitly she had mastered the language through sheer hard work and determination. He looked at his wife. *She's as beautiful as ever.*

Linh eyed her mother's floor-length blue skirt, white shoes, and short-sleeved, red-sequined top. The earrings in the shape of the Statue of Liberty did not go unnoticed, nor did the charm bracelet with the differing landmarks of their adopted country. "Just a bit over the top, Mother, considering the food we're serving," Linh offered drily.

"I think you look splendid, my sweet," Phil said proudly extending his arms to hug her. "This is *your* party, *your* day and you can do what *you* like."

"That's what I thought. After all, I'm an American now." She beamed. "That means I have the freedom to express myself as I please."

They all laughed.

The doorbell rang heralding the arrival of the first guests. Kim-Ly went to greet them, while Phil started the music. He had recorded a special CD of patriotic songs, and the sounds of "America the Beautiful" welcomed the first group of guests. There was much excitement and joy as Kim-Ly welcomed the friends she had made since arriving in America. Many of them were from the hospital where she had worked as a nurse for most of the time.

Their friends continued to arrive, and the party was in full swing. Everyone was savoring the food, and Phil made sure that the hot dog tray was filled, as he boiled more on the stovetop. There was much merriment. After most people had eaten and seemingly enjoyed the buffet, Phil finally stopped the music and drew the crowd's attention. The doorbell rang, and Linh opened the door to let Mark Roades in. She motioned to him to be quiet, as Phil was about to give a toast to his wife.

"Dear Friends," Phil started, his arm around Kim-Ly's shoulders. "Thank you for being here tonight to celebrate my wife's citizenship. I must confess it took Kim to teach me to appreciate America—the country where I have taken so much for granted. Kim was overwhelmed when she came to Las Vegas from Vietnam. It was a huge adjustment for her. Yet, she embraced our country, our culture, and our way of life. It was she who reminded me of the many blessings we have here in America. I'll always be grateful to you for that." Phil looked at Kim-Ly lovingly. Then, as an afterthought, he added somewhat impishly, "Well, that and a few other things." Everyone laughed. "I'm so proud of you," he continued. "And I'm equally proud of my daughter." Phil beckoned Linh to join them. "Thank you, Linh, for taking a few days off from your important work at the United Nations and for flying in from New York to share this special day and be here for the party." The assembled crowd applauded.

"Hey, what was the swearing-in-ceremony like, Kim?" someone from the crowd yelled.

"It was amazing. I have a certificate, and I actually received a letter from the president welcoming me to the United States," she boasted. People gasped in awe. "How many of you here in this room can say you have received a letter from our president?" she continued proudly, as she held it up for all to see. "We all said the Pledge of Allegiance, and they played lots of American songs. It was very solemn, but I enjoyed it very much. All my life, I didn't know anything about "the American Dream," and now, like many immigrants from all over the world, here I am living it." She was radiant as she looked at her husband and daughter. Everyone applauded again, and some whistled loudly expressing their happiness for her.

"Wait here, honey," Phil commanded, as he and Linh disappeared into the kitchen. Hidden in the back was a cake in the shape of the United States. They hurriedly lit a few candles, and Phil carried the cake into the living room, singing "God Bless America" as he went. The guests joined in and a few wiped tears from their eyes as he placed the cake on the coffee table, in the middle of the room.

Kim-Ly blew out the candles, and Linh brought in plates and forks and proceeded to slice the cake, handing out pieces to those nearby, asking them to be passed around. Phil started the music back up and went to see who had arrived as he was about to make his speech.

"Ah, pleased to meet you, Father Roades. Thank you for coming. Let me introduce you to my wife."

"Oh, we can do that shortly," he interjected. "Let your wife enjoy her moment in the spotlight. I am curious, though. Your marriage certificate lists her name as Kim-Ly, yet you called her Kim."

Phil laughed. "Yes, her real name is Kim-Ly. It means Golden Lion. But as she has become more Americanized, she prefers to be called Kim. It's so much easier for everyone."

"And the young lady you introduced, is that your daughter?"

Phil could see the confusion in Mark Roades's eyes. "Yes. I was separated from Kim at the end of the Vietnam conflict. I didn't know Linh existed. She tracked me down. It is a long story, but through my daughter, I reconnected with Kim. Neither of us had married anyone else. When we first reunited, I wondered whether I was in love with just a memory." There was something wistful in his voice.

"In love with a memory of Vietnam?" asked Mark.

"No, not Vietnam. My memories of the loving and comforting times with Kim. My times with her were a touch of sanity in a crazy world. But we're so very happy together now—here." He paused as if lost in thought, and then continued. "Linh means "Gentle Spirit" in Vietnamese. My wife and daughter could also have their names reversed," he chuckled, as he looked on with admiration at his family. "Kim is a gentle and caring spirit. She works at a hospital and is very devoted to her patients. She worries about them and cries when she loses any of them. Linh is indeed a golden lion. She is courageous and fears nothing and no one. I've been truly blessed, Father. And, by the way, talking of blessings I wonder what happened to my good friend, Rosemary?"

"I'm sure she'll be along later. Shortly, after we spoke, she said Buster was not looking well, and she was taking him to the vet. She probably just got a little delayed there."

"I hope nothing happens to that dog. Rosemary would be

devastated. Oh, and what was it you wanted to discuss about Rosemary?"

Mark Roades proceeded to unveil the plans for Rosemary's party.

Phil was excited. "A surprise party. What a fantastic idea. Absolutely, you can count us in. We'll call the Bella Del Mundo when we receive the official invite and tell them. It would be nice if Linh could come, as she was there at our wedding—odd as it sounds. The UN sends her all over the place. We never know where she will be. Maybe she'll be close by and can join us."

"We'll need to come up with a reason as to how I came to be here tonight," Mark said.

"Not a problem. I'll just tell Rosemary that I called to check that she was definitely coming, and you answered the phone, and I invited you. I'm sure the Lord won't mind a little lie under the circumstances." He smiled. "Come, let's get you some food and you can meet Kim and my daughter."

Mark followed the host through the room. Sounds of Lee Greenwood singing "I'm proud to be an American, where at least I know I'm free," started to emanate from the CD player. A couple of people started to sing along. The guests began to link arms, as more and more people joined in.

As the crowd sang heartily and joyously, Phil looked at Kim-Ly who was smiling and seemed so radiantly happy. She was thoroughly enjoying her celebration party and was obviously grateful for her life in her adopted homeland. He wondered whether she ever thought about her prior world in Ho Chi Minh City, now thousands of miles and a lifetime away.

Chapter 17
A Gathering of the Clan

Rosemary knocked on Mark's office door. "Would you mind locking up tonight, Father Mark?" she asked. "I have to take Buster to the vet." The doxie was tired, and immediately curled himself up by her feet, his elongated-knit jacket wrapped around his body, keeping him warm from the cold night air.

Mark looked up from his desk. He had given up asking her to call him by his first name. "No, I don't mind at all. Is Buster's arthritis getting any better?"

"I don't know. I've changed his diet as instructed. Tonight, he's due for his hot tub session. The vet swears it helps the arthritic condition, and Buster loves them. It was my Christmas gift to him … I treated him to six sessions," she admitted, somewhat sheepishly.

Mark opened his drawer and pulled out a little dog biscuit from the bag he kept. He headed around the desk, dropped the biscuit in front of Buster, and bent over to pat the dachshund on his head and stroke his nose. "Oh, and what did he give you for Christmas, Rosemary?" laughed Mark.

"Lots of licks and a lifetime of affection," she chuckled and then became more somber. "But now, with this onset of arthritis, I truly am concerned about how he will cope up north. It's so much colder than it is here, and they have so much snow that seems to last for such a long time. I worry and wonder if I'm being fair to him."

Mark smiled at her. "Well, you still have a couple of weeks to see if the hot tub sessions work. How's the packing going?"

"Oh, don't ask. Didn't realize I was such a pack rat. Well, goodnight, Father Mark."

"Goodnight, Rosemary. God Bless."

His phone rang. "Good evening, Chapel of Eternal Love, Father Mark Roades speaking."

"Good evening, Mark. Belated Happy New Year to you. This is Chad and Pru Nelson calling."

"And Happy New Year back to you both. Your timing couldn't be more perfect. Rosemary just left for the evening."

"Well, it's only two weeks until her event, and we thought we should compare notes so we can plan seating and have an accurate head count. I'll tell you who we have registered for rooms and who responded to the invite. There are probably a few who gave you a verbal response, as well," Chad continued.

Mark pulled a folder from his desk drawer. "Okay, I have my list. Who do you have on yours?"

"We have a group of six adults with two children coming from Tennessee. They have booked three rooms."

"Ah, yes. They run an Elvis online memorabilia store. Two sets of parents and their married children, and now grandchildren. Three adult couples all got married at the chapel. Can you believe that? " Mark chuckled. "They've all reserved the last appointment on Rosemary's last day to renew their wedding vows. It will be thirty years for both sets of the in-laws and five years for Elvis and Cilla—that's the name of the couple who actually married that day."

"Wow, I bet they have a story. Unbelievable. Since they're all obviously a close family we'll put them at one table." While they were talking, Pru started her seating chart. "We also have a couple from Hawaii flying in and Congresswoman Maxwell and her husband from Texas," Chad said.

Mark looked through his notes. "Right, the two from Hawaii are Julian and Hayley. They run an orchid farm and own a couple of florists. Congresswoman Maxwell wasn't sure about their coming, so I'm glad her husband confirmed with you."

Pru was scribbling the names and notes for the seating plan. "If she's a member of Congress, maybe they should sit with us at the head table. We're planning on six or eight per table, depending on the final count. Rosemary will obviously sit with the three of us and perhaps they could round out the number with another couple."

"Actually, there's a single lady who I would like to sit with us if possible. That is, if you don't mind," said Mark.

"Maybe, we can just get the total guests and see that we're on the same page with Mark, then you can do the seating plan later, honey," Chad suggested, slightly agitated they weren't staying on focus. "But since we're talking of single ladies, we have one coming from Mississippi. Her name is Mattie Bridges. I don't know why she's solo. I didn't want to ask her."

"Oh, that pleases me," said Mark. "At least, it pleases me that she's attending. When I contacted them, Mattie wasn't sure. Her husband was killed in a motorcycle accident just before Thanksgiving. She has a baby not yet six months old. Very sad. I never heard back, but she obviously called you."

"Yes, she was very concerned about the babysitting

services. She's planning on staying quite a few days. I think she may be looking to move here. She did seem pretty distraught, though."

"That's tragic and heartbreaking. Maybe *she* can sit at our table," said Pru. Chad cast a slightly disapproving glance at her. "Sorry, Chad. Who else do we have, honey?"

"There's one couple driving up from Pomona, California and staying the night. Guess one of the sets of in-laws is coming with them to babysit because they reserved two rooms."

"Yes, I have them on my list. That's Jenny and Derek. It's good they're coming. She didn't know if it would be in their budget. They're young and paying their own way through college."

"That's all we have coming long distance. Locally, I heard from Giovanni and Becky Largenti."

"Oh, I think that's the Jewish and Catholic couple. I happened to call them when they were having a Hanukkah and Christmas dinner with both sets of parents. It didn't sound as if it was going so well." Mark laughed, recalling how Becky had invited him over in case he was needed to perform last rites in the event she killed one of the parents.

"I also received a written note from a Sarah Windmeyer. It was difficult to read. Judging by the handwriting, I think she's fairly elderly. She mentioned her husband is in a memory care facility, but thought it might be good for him to get out. She said you told her you could provide transportation for them if necessary."

"Yes, I did. I'm thrilled she's coming. She sounded very doubtful on the phone and didn't seem receptive to the idea of bringing her husband. But I've had a few conversations with her since. She must have had a change of heart. Emmy said she would collect them if necessary. I'll follow up on that."

"Who's Emmy?" Chad asked. "I don't have her on my list."

"That's because I didn't send you her address for an invite. She's the lady I was mentioning who I'd like to sit at our table, if possible. I'm trying to talk her into taking Rosemary's job. I haven't found a replacement yet."

"Well, what about her husband? Isn't he coming?" Pru inquired.

"Actually, he stood her up at the altar that day. She'll be coming alone."

"That *is* sad. How can people be so cruel?" Pru asked.

Chad was engrossed sorting through his list and missed the comments about Emmy. "We also received a reply from a Peter and Renee Sharpstone and two couples with the name Mr. and Mrs. Roscoe."

"Peter and Renee are owners of the *Repent* perfume line. She's known by her maiden name, Renee Kingsgate. I'm sure you've seen the TV commercials. The Roscoe's are two sets of twins. You'll need name tags for Chester and Dolly and Lester and Molly."

"Got it. Okay. That's all I have. Oh, and of course, Rosa De La Corazon and her husband. They're coming."

"Rosa's bringing her husband?" asked Pru.

"Well, it seemed appropriate she bring him. We discussed it when she came to see me just before Christmas," Chad replied.

"I have a couple more that contacted me and evidently didn't notify you," Mark said looking through his notes. "There's a Taylor and Sherri. They're a local couple. And then there's Phil, Kim, and their daughter, Linh." He spelled Linh's name out for Pru."

"That's an unusual spelling. I've never seen it spelled like that before," said Pru.

"It's Vietnamese. Phil's wife is from Vietnam. They're friends of Rosemary's and the people whose home we're going to for dinner the last night."

"Interesting, there are no divorces," Pru observed. "And here I thought we'd be the only ones still married, Chad." She smiled and laughed softly.

"Since you mentioned it, you didn't hear from a Mitch or Diana Barlow, did you?" asked Mark.

"Wait a minute," Chad said. "Yes. Now, where's their card?" He rummaged through the pile. "Here it is. Mitch Barlow called and confirmed, then his wife called and cancelled. Then, Mitch called again and reconfirmed and reserved a room for the night. Sounds like there are some issues there."

Praise be to God, Mark thought. *Maybe that marriage can be salvaged after all.*

"Not necessarily, dear," responded Pru. "Have you been in touch with Pastor Glen during all this, Mark?"

"I've called him off and on. He's excited to hear of all the details, and asks lots of questions."

"I suppose we should have invited him," Pru pondered.

"That's a good idea. It's not too late, you know," Chad said.

Mark imagined what the journey would be like for the elder minister. "I think it would be too much for him to travel now. Don't think he could make it to the airports, the changing of planes, or going through security, and all that traveling now entails."

Pru reached for her lighter and lit a cigarette. "We could send a limo and put him up in one of our resorts in Salt Lake City to split the journey up. Then, it would not be too long of a drive for him. Why don't you give him a call, Mark? See what he says."

"That's extraordinarily kind and generous of you. It's probably too late to contact him tonight. I'll call him in the morning."

Chad was cross checking his list. "Well, I've added Emmy. Wow! Mattie Bridges husband aside, it looks as if we have a perfect attendance."

"No, wait," said Mark. "What happened about the couple you were going to speak to your private eye about? The one I didn't have any address or contact information for. His name was Cory Moran and hers was Samantha Jameson. Those are the only two who are unaccounted for."

"Oh, sorry about that. Yes, I did hear from the investigator. He was able to find absolutely nothing on either of these individuals. Zip, zilch, nada," Chad said. "They've vanished into thin air. I was told these two either gave fictitious names for some reason, or they were in the witness protection program, living in some remote and secluded location." He laughed at the prospect.

Chapter 18

A Quiet, Simple Life

"Adios, Señor," yelled the last of the children as they ran down the stairs from the small schoolhouse, books tucked haphazardly under their arms.

"*Mañana*," Cory called after them. "Don't forget to do your homework."

It was midafternoon and a very warm day, even for January—the heart of summer in the southern hemisphere. Cory took the short drive in his dilapidated car from the village to his modest lakeside home in Chile Chico, the little town in northern Patagonia, Chile, a few miles west of the Argentinean border.

He stopped by the post office to collect the mail and was surprised to see an official looking letter from the United States Government addressed to his wife. *Now what?* he thought. *Heidi is totally settled and does not need any more updates on the status of the creep who put her through such a terrible ordeal.* It had been nine years since she'd been in the witness protection program for being a firsthand observer to a murder. The murderer, who Heidi had identified, had been found guilty but had been through every appeal afforded him. Each time, the government saw fit to keep the couple updated. Cory resented that the letter was addressed to *Samantha*, the new name given

Heidi once she entered the witness protection program.

"Heidi, I'm home," Cory called out loudly. He'd always insisted on referring to her by her real name.

"I'm in the garden," she shouted back, continuing to tug at the weeds. She looked up and, on observing the serious look on his face, asked "What's the matter?"

He handed her the letter. She removed her gardening gloves, mopped her brow, and sat on the swing they had placed in the garden for their daughter, Courtney, when she was younger. Heidi opened the letter and read it slowly. Cory was watching for a reaction.

Finally, Heidi gripped the letter firmly in one hand, the other flew to her mouth covering it as she sobbed uncontrollably.

Cory rushed to her side. "What is it? What is it?" He placed his arm protectively around her. She handed him the letter.

"He's dead. He's actually dead," she said between sobs. "I can finally live in peace, and without fear. My nightmare is over."

Cory read the letter and took a few seconds to digest it. "How ironic the sleazebag was finally sent to prison, only to be murdered by a fellow inmate. But, what of the other robber? I wonder where he is?"

"Remember, I told you, he was given life imprisonment and committed suicide."

"That's right. I forgot." He continued to hug his wife while stroking her hair, allowing her to cry until she was emotionally drained.

Wiping her face, she looked up at him. "The letter says we

can go home at last, and I can finally see my mother, *if* we can find her."

"I'm sure the folks at witness protection can help. There's a number here we can call. Why don't you let me call them while you go and pick up Courtney?"

"Oh, Courtney is spending the night at Fabiana's. They're having a slumber party," she chuckled. "Don't worry, it's supervised."

"Then, since it's just you and I, why don't we celebrate? We can have dinner at our favorite restaurant down by the lake. You go up and change, let me call America."

"I know why I love you and why I married you." She kissed her husband and hurriedly ran upstairs while Cory made his call.

Heidi returned wearing a woven cotton wrap skirt with a bright-green blouse and large, red bangle earrings.

Cory smiled. "You're looking your South American best."

Holding hands, they left the house and strolled along the lakefront promenade to their destination, while he gave her the details of his phone conversation with the witness protection program.

"But how do they know my mom moved to Las Vegas? I never thought she would leave Salt Lake City. I just don't believe it."

"Well, I guess the agency can track people using the social security numbers and linking through the IRS. Who knows? But they have powers and information that we clearly don't have access to. Maybe your stepfather got a job in Vegas." He shrugged. "Anyway, the agency is going to see if they can get your mom's phone number. We can call them tomorrow."

They arrived at the restaurant and were seated by a window overlooking the lake. Since it was summer, even though it was late afternoon, the sun was still high in the clear blue sky. They watched the fishing boats drifting across the still lake and some of the young children playing in the sand on the tiny beach close-by. They ordered their dinner and cocktails.

Heidi adopted a serious tone. "I really do need to go back as soon as possible. I truly miss having not been able to see my mom." Her eyes welled up again.

He reached across the table. "I'll speak to the school tomorrow. They can get a substitute in for a couple of weeks." He tried to perk her up a little. "Hey, you know that also in a couple of weeks it will be our fifth wedding anniversary? Remember that cute little wedding chapel where we got married?"

Heidi nodded.

"Maybe, we can plan our trip to be there in time for our anniversary. Perhaps, we can renew our wedding vows? Your folks can join us, since they couldn't attend the wedding."

"How romantic. You always know just what to say and do to make things right. I love you for that." She shook her head as she squeezed his hand.

Their Pisco sour cocktails arrived along with a platter of rainbow trout beautifully decorated with alternating lemon and tomato wedges.

After dinner, they walked slowly home, arm in arm. Cory pondered what this latest turn of events would do for their long-term future. Patagonia had captured his soul years earlier after he'd completed his second mission. He knew Heidi was happy but was always aware how she yearned for her homeland.

As if reading his mind, she said, "You know, this really has me in a turmoil. All these years I've longed to go home to Salt Lake City or even back to Alaska. Have looked forward to that day since we left America. And yet, now the realization is settling in, I am beginning to think of what I'll be leaving behind. The quiet, simple and uncomplicated life we have here. The peaceful feeling of waking up and looking out over this beautiful serene lake. Courtney is so happy here and loves her classmates and pals. Chile Chico and our friends in the Mormon church, have embraced us. Everyone's been so accepting. My heart is torn."

Cory stopped and looked at her. "I'd always hoped Patagonia would capture your heart and mind the way it captured mine. It's been the perfect retreat for us given the circumstances. But I don't want to pressure you, either. A decision doesn't have to be made now. Let's go back to see your mom and stepfather and see how things lie."

"And don't forget … go back to renew our wedding vows," she grinned. "I guess a lot will have changed in America."

"Oh, I don't know. Probably not," Cory responded. "It will always be the good old USA. But you have changed—and that will be the key. Let's wait until we get back before making a final decision. Okay?"

She nodded and smiled. "Sounds like a plan."

"I promise you, Mom, we won't be gone for long," Heidi said, hugging her mother. "We just want to make a quick trip to the chapel to see if they can fit us in tomorrow to renew our wedding vows. While we're gone, it will give you some precious time with Courtney."

Cory honked the car horn.

"Coming," she yelled and ran toward their rented car.

"It sure is nice to see you and your mom spend time together. There's so much to catch up on," Cory said as she climbed in the car.

They talked continuously as they made their way and were excited to see the *Chapel of Eternal Love* wedding sign they both remembered so well.

"I wonder if the lady and her little dog will still be there," Cory said.

Both were surprised, as well as disappointed, to see an unfamiliar minister behind the counter in the office. "I know it's late in the day, Father," Cory said. "But is there a time tomorrow we could come and renew our wedding vows?"

"How special," smiled Mark, "and refreshing to hear." He looked in the book. "Actually, it looks as if tomorrow is pretty booked. How about Monday? We have some time available then."

Heidi and Cory were crestfallen. Heidi pleaded, "Isn't there even a ten minute slot somewhere during the day? You see, this weekend is our fifth anniversary, and we were married right here in this chapel. There was a lady who worked here at the time. She had a cute, friendly little dachshund."

"Oh, that's Rosemary. She's still here. She just left early today to take her dog to the vet. He has some health issues." Suddenly, it dawned on Mark, who this couple might be. "Say, your names aren't Cory and Samantha are they?"

Cory and Heidi looked at each other. Cory was a little

Return to the Chapel of Eternal Love

suspicious. *How would he know our names, especially after five years?* "That's an odd question," he said without revealing anything.

"Well, tomorrow is Rosemary's last day. We're having a surprise farewell party for her this evening at the new Bella Del Mundo hotel and resort. We've spent the last month tracking down and inviting everyone who was married exactly five years ago tomorrow. Cory and Samantha were the only couple we couldn't locate. We wondered whether you ... or they ... had escaped from the planet."

Cory and Heidi exchanged glances again and burst out laughing. "Yes, we are those missing persons. And no, we haven't escaped the planet. We've just been in South America," Cory said.

Mark was astounded. "I've said it before, and I'll say it again, God works in mysterious ways. Would you be able to make the party?"

Heidi did a double take. "Well, my mom probably won't be too happy. I think they were hoping we'd spend the night with them. But I'm sure, given the circumstances, they'll understand."

Mark was confused but let the matter go. "I'll call Pru and Chad—they're the hosts, and ask them to set up two more seats. The party is going to be held in the Celebration Room, and everyone is to be there at six-thirty. Chad is collecting Rosemary and will have her there at seven. She thinks she is having a quiet dinner with Pru and Chad—her longtime friends. It promises to be a real nice evening."

Cory looked at his watch. "Wow! We'd better get back home in a hurry and change if we need to be there by six-thirty." He grabbed Heidi's hand and headed for the car.

Heidi was pensive during the ride back in the car.

"A penny for your thoughts?" Cory teased.

"Well, I know we've only been back here for two days. It's wonderful to see Mom and Arthur, and it's great to be back in the USA, but my heart is already pining for Chile Chico. Who would have thought I'd ever be homesick for Patagonia?"

"I would," Cory responded as he removed a hand from the steering wheel and placed it over hers.

As they arrived back at Heidi's parents, Courtney came running out to meet them. "Mommy, Daddy, when are we going home? I want to go home."

"What's up, precious? Don't you like seeing your grandma?" Heidi asked.

Courtney pouted. "Yes, but I miss my friends. I want to go home."

Cory and Heidi looked at each other and smiled. "I guess the decision is made," he said to his wife as he stretched out his arms for a group hug. He kissed Courtney on the head. "We'll be going home soon, baby, real soon."

Chapter 19

Surprise!

"It's so kind of you to fetch Oscar and me and take us to the party," Sarah said to Emmy, as they headed toward the memory care facility where Oscar now lived.

The rain was coming down in torrents, and the windshield wipers of Emmy's car were racing back and forth. "Not a problem," replied Emmy as she pulled into the parking lot and stopped beneath the awning at the entrance. "I'll come in with you, in case you need any help."

"Thank you. You're so very thoughtful. It's such a comfort having you with me. This will be the first time my husband has been out of the building since he moved here. I don't know how he'll be. Staff said they would have him all dressed and ready."

Emmy smiled. "I'm sure he'll be fine. Don't worry." *I wonder how much he has changed since the days when he was a client at my agency?*

They made their way into the reception area of the building where a caregiver was sitting next to Oscar, holding his hand. Oscar's other hand was clutching the armrest of his wheelchair.

Sarah beamed. *My, he looks so dapper in his jacket and tie.* She leaned over and gave her husband a kiss. "Oscar, this is Emmy. She's taking us to the party."

Oscar grinned at Emmy, as she reached out and touched his hands. His eyes twinkled.

Sarah was astounded. "Good heavens, it's almost as if he knows you. As if he recognizes you." She really looked at Emmy for the first time. "Of course, I remember now. You were sitting at the back of the chapel the day we married. I thought I'd seen you somewhere before when I met you earlier tonight. I just couldn't place the face."

Emmy deftly changed the subject. "Why don't you let me push the chair to the car? You can sit in the back seat. It might be better for you to be there with him."

As they headed toward the entrance, the sound of a paramedic van and fire engine could be heard entering the driveway.

"Darn, they've blocked my exit," said Emmy as she observed one of the vans pulling in front of her car and one behind her. "I hope this doesn't make us too late for the party."

At the Bella Del Mundo's Celebration Room, Pru was hastily re-arranging the seating at the tables in light of Cory and Heidi, the two last minute additions. *Forty people. What a perfect size for an intimate gathering.* Even though there were four tables with eight place settings, and her table with only six, it would now be perfect with Cory and Heidi rounding out the group. *Probably makes sense to now have the elderly couple at our table,* she thought. She moved Sarah and Oscar's name tags to her table and shifted a couple of the other tags around. *Not knowing these people, I hope I have placed the guests with the people they will like.*

She returned to the doorway, looked at the room in front of her, and smiled. *Chad's made good on his promise. Everything looks just as it should.* She noticed the perfectly arranged settings on the pink tablecloths and the napkins folded on the china plates, in the shape of hearts, neatly positioned in front of the crystal stemware. *Champagne flutes, wine, and water glasses all perfectly symmetrical. The orchid centerpieces are absolutely stunning.* She turned her eyes to the stage and saw the band instruments all set and ready. The large banner proclaiming *Good Luck Rosemary and Buster* hung from the ceiling.

"Excuse me. Is it too soon to come in?" Bobby said from behind.

Pru turned around and smiled. She was in her element at these events. "Not at all. Please do." She extended her hand. "I'm Pru Nelson. My husband and I are your hosts for the evening."

"My name's Bobby. This is my wife, Mavis; our best friends, Val and Mike; and my son and daughter-in-law, Elvis and Cilla. We're here from Tennessee."

"Ah yes," replied Pru. You're the group who had Kid Galahad, the Elvis impersonator, perform at your wedding. I hear you've asked him to sing again when you renew your vows tomorrow."

"Gee, that's amazing. How did you know?" Val asked.

Pru smiled. "I guess you told him you were coming back for Rosemary's retirement party. He knows her quite well from the services he's performed at the chapel over the years. So he's asked if he could come and sing this evening as a guest spot. Said there would be no charge; it would be a parting gift for Rosemary."

Cilla bounced up and down a little, and giggled with excitement, as she clapped her hands together softly. "Wow, I can't believe it. We'll see Kid Galahad tonight as well as tomorrow."

"Calm down, honey. Keep your cool," Elvis chided. He turned to Pru. "Mighty awesome place you and your husband have here, Ma'am. Talking of gifts, is there a gift table? We have a little something for Rosemary, too."

Pru pointed to a nearby table against the wall. "Thank you. Let me show you where you'll be sitting." Pru led them to their assigned table on the other side of the dance floor. "I've placed you with a couple who live here locally. I'm sure they can answer any questions you have about Las Vegas." She heard voices and turned to see who they were. "Oh, I see other guests arriving, and thank goodness, the members of the band are here. Excuse me," she said to the Elvis lovers, "let me go and greet them. I'm sure we'll chat later."

"Good evening, I'm Pru Nelson." She extended her hand to the couple standing at the entrance. *What a sweet-looking young couple,* she thought. *But so very young.*

"I'm Derek, and this is my wife, Betty-Sue."

"You're the owner of this hotel, right?" asked Betty-Sue, in a somewhat coy manner.

"That's right, my dear, along with my husband, Chad. Thank you for coming."

"I think your decorations and designs are just gorgeous. Simply magnificent," Betty-Sue said.

Derek put his arm around Betty-Sue's shoulder. "My wife is studying to be an interior designer. She loves all these kind of things."

"Well, good for you, Betty-Sue. When you graduate, maybe you can come and work for us?" Pru suggested. She pointed to a table. "You're at the table next to where the group of six is seated on the other side of the dance floor. "Please enjoy yourselves and your stay with us."

Derek dropped off a wrapped gift at what he assumed was the gift table.

The two sets of twins, Lester and Molly and Chester and Dolly appeared at the door along with several of the other guests. Pru was relieved to see Mark Roades arrive with Pastor Glen, holding onto his arm. She beckoned him to the front.

"Since Chad has gone to collect Rosemary, could you please help me welcome and seat the guests? You and Pastor Glen are seated at Table One over there."

"Sure. Let me seat Glen, and I'll be back to help you." The elder pastor moved very slowly as Mark walked him to the table, after which Mark returned to assist Pru.

Lester looked at their seating assignments. Chester and Dolly were on the left, while Lester and Molly were on the right. "Can't have that," said Lester, quickly switching the name tags around. "Nobody but us will know the difference. We all know I have to be on the left and Chester on the right."

Mark was standing by the door when Sherri and Taylor arrived each holding a package. One was a beautifully wrapped box, the other a basket wrapped in cellophane filled with assorted dog treats and toys. A big note was attached at the top saying, "For Buster."

"Very thoughtful of you," Mark smiled. "Rosemary will appreciate it as I'm sure Buster will."

"I just love dogs. Always have, always will," Taylor

said. Sherri was feeling uneasy, as she eyed the other ladies present—sizing up their hairstyles, makeup and attire. Sensing her discomfort, Taylor linked their arms and patted her hand for reassurance.

"Looks like that's the table for the gifts," said Mark, pointing to where other gifts had been placed. Then please find your seats."

Not exactly what I had in mind when I asked him to help, thought Pru. *But I guess it doesn't hurt. At least, he can welcome some of the guests.*

"We're Julian and Hayley," said Julian, holding hands with his wife.

"I'm Pru and you must be the couple from Hawaii."

"That's right." Julian smiled, showing his white teeth and dimples.

"The orchids you sent for the centerpieces are truly spectacular. Thank you so much for your generosity." She watched them turn to each other and give reciprocal loving glances. *What a beautiful couple these two are, and clearly so much in love,* thought Pru.

Mark was greeting Mitch and Diana. Mitch spotted the table holding the packages and rushed to put their contribution among the others. He quickly darted around the tables to see where they were to sit.

"Thank you so much for coming," said Mark as he shook Diana's hand profusely, pulling her to the one side. "I do hope you'll consider joining Mitch and me at our sessions. I believe we're making real progress."

He's certainly much younger than I imagined, and clearly more progressive, thought Diana as she looked at the minister. "I'll definitely think about it, Father. I'm already seeing a difference in Mitch. Thank you. My husband has not had a drink in over a month now."

"Your husband is a good man, Diana."

She wondered exactly how much her husband had told Mark about their matrimonial problems.

Pru recognized the next two couples coming through the door. "I just adore your perfume," she said as she shook Renee and Peter's hands, and turning to the next couple, "I appreciate your coming, Congresswoman Maxwell. And I certainly thank you for your service, Mr. Maxwell," not commenting on his limp and cane. Pru had followed their stories on the news. "You're all sitting at the same table, so I hope you enjoy yourselves. Are those for Rosemary?" she asked, noting the gifts in the ladies' hands. Both women nodded. "Let me take them," Pru added. "You're seated right here." She patted the chair at the table closest to her.

Rosa appeared at the door, with her husband, holding her wrapped gift box. "Señora Nelson, this my husband, Ernesto," she beamed.

"Thank you for help, Señora Nelson. My wife, she say how kind you are." Ernesto clasped Pru's hand with both of his. "We are so grateful."

Pru smiled at them. "You look so radiant tonight, Rosa. That fresh plumeria in your hair looks so pretty. Please, join that lovely young couple over there." She pointed to Derek and Betty-Sue. "I have also seated you next to a couple who are here from South America. I know it's a long way from Guatemala, but thought you might enjoy their company."

Meanwhile, Mark was greeting Becky and Giovanni. "Ah,

I remember chatting with you briefly when you were having a family gathering for Hanukkah and Christmas. You seemed a little stressed," he laughed.

"You don't want to know, Father. You really don't," joked Becky. "Where are we sitting?" Mark directed them to Derek and Betty-Sue's table.

Mattie walked in at the same time as Phil, Kim-Ly, and their daughter Linh. Pru thought they were together.

"No, I'm by myself," said Mattie. *I really shouldn't have come here tonight. What in the world made me come all this way?*

Pru realized immediately who it was and asked Mark to guide the other three guests to their table. Instinctively, she put her arms around Mattie to give her a warm and welcome hug. "Thank you so much for coming, my dear. I am so sorry for your loss. If there is anything my husband and I can do to make your stay with us more pleasant, don't hesitate to let us know."

Mattie instantly felt at ease. "Thank you so much. Judging by my accommodations, I don't think that will be necessary. I'm sure I won't want for anything," she laughed, somewhat nervously.

"I know you'll find the company at your table very interesting. Let me introduce you." She took her to where Phil, Kim-Ly, and Linh had just seated themselves. At the same table were Peter and Renee and Congresswoman Maxwell and Kurt.

The last couple, just scraping under the wire before six-thirty, was Cory and Heidi. Mark greeted them at the door.

"I hope we're not too late, Father," said Cory, a little out of breath and looking at his watch.

"You're here, that's all that matters. The guest of honor should be arriving any moment." He took them to the only two seats left, next to Rosa and Ernesto, and returned to take his seat at the main table.

Hmm, he thought, looking at the two vacant seats across the table and the empty chair next to him. *I wonder what has happened to Emmy, Sarah, and Oscar?*

As if reading his mind, Pru took a sip from her glass of water and observed, "Looks like everyone is here except your lady friend and the couple she was picking up. I do hope nothing has happened to them?"

"So do I," said Mark.

Pru's cell phone rang. She did not answer, as she knew it was Chad's cue that the guest of honor was approaching. She quickly alerted the assembled crowd to stand up and to shout the word "surprise" when Rosemary entered.

The door of the Celebration Room opened, and Chad walked in with Rosemary on his arm. Buster was trotting beside her at the end of the leash she held in her other hand.

"Surprise!" yelled everyone and gave way to a round of applause.

Chapter 20

Party Time

The band started to play, but Rosemary didn't hear a note. She observed the *Good Luck Rosemary and Buster* sign hanging from the ceiling, looked at the sea of vaguely familiar smiling faces in front of her, and realized the party was in her honor.

"Oh, my goodness, I'm not properly dressed for this," she exclaimed, clasping her face in surprise and dropping Buster's leash at the same time. The assembled group laughed and cheered.

Buster seized the moment and hobbled, dragging his leash, to the table where Sherri and Taylor were seated, the arthritis in his back legs causing him difficulty. He could smell dog lovers a mile away, and enjoyed the scents of other dogs as he sniffed around their feet. Taylor bent over to pat him and unfastened the restraint.

"Buster, come back her at once," Rosemary called after him. Everyone chuckled. He headed back toward his mistress, stopping at the table where Kurt Maxwell was seated. The dog sat down beside his chair and looked up respectfully, as if paying homage to the veteran. He then trotted along the table to Phil and wagged his tail. Since Rosemary had been long time friends of Phil, Buster was very familiar with him, but he started to sneeze being so close to Renee, smelling the scent of her perfume. Peter rose from his seat next to his wife, and started clicking away with his camera. As designated photographer for the evening, he was determined to make his souvenir picture album for Rosemary a memorable one.

Chad signaled to the band to stop playing. "It will be five years ago tomorrow that we were all married at the Chapel of Eternal Love," he announced, placing his arm around Rosemary's shoulder. "All of us, that is, except Father Mark Roades and the founder of the chapel, Pastor Glen." The elder minister stood up and waved. "Not forgetting, of course, the heart of the chapel, our guest of honor, Rosemary and little Buster." Tears of joy started to flow down Rosemary's cheeks as Mark came and guided her to the table and seated her between himself and Pastor Glen. Surprised to see the pastor, Rosemary gave him a warm hug.

"Many of you have traveled a great distance to be here, and we welcome you to Las Vegas and to our tribute to Rosemary. Dinner will now be served, to be followed by dancing and celebration," Chad announced, and headed to the table to join his wife and the other guests.

No sooner had he sat down, when Emmy appeared pushing Oscar in the wheelchair with one hand, and holding Sarah by the arm with the other. On seeing all the gifts, she quickly stopped by, opened her purse, and placed a small wrapped box on the table.

Mark realized who she was and rose to greet her. "You haven't returned my calls about taking Rosemary's place at the chapel," he chided her with a gentle voice.

"Nobody can take Rosemary's place, Father," she replied with a smile. "I'm so sorry we're late. We had a slight delay at the home when we picked up Oscar."

Mark led them to the table, where they were all seated. Emmy helped Oscar out of his wheelchair and into the dining chair, before Mark introduced the three new arrivals to the rest of the guests. Chad's face turned ashen. There was a time in his gigolo past when he had worked for Emmy—a time in his life of which he was not too proud. He wondered whether Emmy would let on. True to form, as experience had taught her, she shook his hand providing no hint of prior acknowledgement. Pru on the other hand, recognized that knowing look in Chad's eyes, but chose to ignore it. Emmy and Rosemary hugged each other.

"I have wondered about you so often, my dear," said Rosemary. "How have you been?"

Emmy smiled. "I've been fine, thank you. Your boss here has been trying to hire me for when you leave."

"Not with any degree of success, I might add," interjected Mark, as he introduced her to Pastor Glen. *Probably the only time in my life I will be seated at a table with not only one man of the cloth, but two,* thought Emmy. She smiled at the irony. Buster sniffed at her feet and licked her legs. She stooped down to stroke his forehead. Looking around the room, she recognized Giovanni and his wife and waved to them. *I wonder if he's still styling hair. I should probably visit him again.*

Rosemary was doing some recollections of her own. The faces were all familiar, but she struggled to remember her part in any of the ceremonies. Of course, the Elvis clan was easy to recall, as were the twins. It was the only time she had seen two sets of twins. She recognized Renee and Peter, while remembering receiving the bottle of perfume from Renee— something she would never have been able to purchase. The ceremony of Kathleen and Kurt was recalled. It was not easy to forget how Kathleen was in such a panic on her wedding day with her plane arriving late. She waved to Phil, Kim-Ly, and Linh, knowing they were hosting a dinner party for her the next evening.

Rosemary nudged Mark and quietly asked, "There's a lady at the table with my friend Phil, and his wife. I vaguely remember her face, but where's her husband?"

"That's Mattie Bridges. She runs a Harley Davidson shop in Mississippi. Sadly, her husband was killed just before Thanksgiving. She's considering moving here to start a new life."

"Oh, that's right. I remember her now. How depressed she must be. Yet, she came all this way. How nice."

As if there was telepathy in the room, Renee struck up a conversation with Mattie. Renee knew her husband would be gone for much of the evening taking photographs. "Well, my husband has a date with his camera this evening," she joked. "What's yours up to?"

Mattie recognized Renee from the commercials and certainly her distinctive, husky, voice. She bit her lip, clutched her napkin, and fought back the tears. "Sadly, I lost my husband last year. He was killed in an accident." Pre-empting Renee's next question, Mattie continued. "I run a Harley Davidson repair shop in Jackson, Mississippi. I'm thinking of selling it. I need to make a move and start fresh somewhere with my young son. I thought I'd spend a few days here in Las Vegas. See what it's like."

Renee instinctively put out her arms to comfort her, wondering how Mattie found the strength to come so far to the party.

"Well, there is a Harley store here. We know the owner and could certainly get you an introduction. What exactly do you do in your repair shop?"

Mattie immediately perked up. "Thank you. Gee, I would certainly appreciate the introduction. My husband had a small group of mechanics. I handled all the office administration: the payroll, all the accounting, filing of taxes, ordering of the parts. You know, all the things necessary for the cogs to turn."

Renee looked at this pretty young lady with her fair complexion and with such sadness in her eyes. *This meeting could be a true blessing,* she thought, as the obvious sprang to her mind. "I'll tell you what," she said excitedly. "My husband, Peter, has been looking for someone to handle much of the administration in our company. Unless you are sold on working in the Harley business, maybe you would consider applying with *Repent.* Peter can see you Monday morning. He'll need someone experienced." She announced with pride, "I'm expecting our first child, and I know he'll be taking a lot of time off work to be with me. He's already overloaded."

The possibilities raced through Mattie's mind, as she thought of a future in the beauty industry. "I'd love to discuss this with your husband on Monday. Wow! Thank you. It sounds like a terrific opportunity."

Renee smiled. "I think we're going to be great friends."

From her vantage point, Rosemary observed Mattie and Renee chatting. It made her happy to see everyone conversing and apparently having a good time. She continued to scan the room, and noticed Betty-Sue and Derek. *Oh, how I remember those two. I'll have to catch up with them later.* She turned back to Pru and Chad. "I can't believe you did all this for me. How can I ever thank you? It's wonderful. Just wonderful."

Pru patted her husband's hand. "Well, Chad did much of the planning, and none of it would have been possible without Mark here, and by all accounts, your meticulous records." They all laughed.

"I can't take credit for the flowers, though," corrected Chad. "The orchid centerpieces were all provided by the couple at the table with the twins. They run an orchid farm in Hawaii."

Rosemary looked and recognized Julian and Hayley. "I remember them well. I played at their wedding. If memory serves, they requested "An Affair to Remember." Seems it had special significance for them. The flowers are beautiful."

The waiters were placing the salads at all the tables, as Chad monitored the service to ensure all guests received their food and beverages at the same time.

"Here, let me help," said Emmy to Sarah, as she got up from her seat and tried to tuck the napkin into Oscar's shirt. Rosemary noted the care which Emmy showed and observed how she had helped Sarah with her husband getting him into the dining chair.

"You'd be perfect for the job at the chapel, Emmy. What's holding you back? If you're not doing anything tomorrow, I could show you the ropes. I'm always available at the end of the phone."

"I agree," offered Pastor Glen. "You have such a caring and giving nature. It's obvious, you're a natural."

Emmy paused for a moment. She was reluctant to take the position at the chapel, wondering whether the daily reminder of her being left at the altar would really help with her pain.

Yet, the warmth and affection she was feeling in this room, made her realize that her secluded life was not a bed of roses, either. There was also something she found very endearing about Mark. "Okay, Mark Roades. I'll tell you what," she said. "I'll come and work for you for three months. We'll see how it goes. If you find someone else in the meantime, they can start. If after three months, I don't like the position, I'll leave. No hard feelings either way. Is it a deal?"

Mark heaved a sigh of relief. "It's a deal."

Pru graciously raised her glass and offered a toast, and everyone clinked their wine glasses. As if on cue, Buster pricked up his ears, left his spot next to Rosemary, made his way around the table, and nestled himself at Emmy's feet.

"Buster, come back here," Rosemary demanded.

"He's no trouble," laughed Emmy, putting an arm down and stroking his ear. "Are you taking him with you when you move?"

"Actually, I've been trying to find a home for him here. His arthritis is getting really bad, especially in his hind legs. I'm concerned about what the weather will be like for him up north with all the snow. It will be heart-wrenching to part with him, but I must put his welfare ahead of my own joy."

"There's a dog lover here," said Pru. "The gentleman who Buster made a beeline toward when you first arrived. There's a big basket on the gift table over there marked "For Buster." It has all kinds of doggie treats. The same gentleman placed it there."

"That's Taylor and his wife, Sherri," said Mark.

"Why give him to another home?" asked Emmy. "My sense is, Buster belongs to the chapel." She felt the dog thumping his tail against her feet. "I'd be more than happy to take him. That way he can go to the chapel every day and be some company for me, while he spends his days in a familiar environment." Emmy remembered how comforting he was at the chapel on her wedding day, when she was at her lowest.

Rosemary was amazed. "You'd give my Buster a home?"

Emmy shrugged. "Sure, why not? Why don't I take him with me tonight? I'll take the basket of dog snacks for food, and we'll see how he settles in. I'll bring him to the chapel tomorrow, so the transition will be a gradual one."

Rosemary started to cry again. "You truly are a godsend, Emmy," she said.

"I would agree," said Mark. "Thank you. You're right. In many ways, Buster *is* part of the chapel."

I don't think I have ever been considered a godsend to anyone, thought Emmy, as once again she considered the irony of her situation.

Conversation could be heard over the clatter of the salad plates being collected by the waiters. Wine glasses were being filled, and the servers arrived with the main course. Everyone seemed to be having a good time.

The party was in full swing and the band played on.

Chapter 21

Return to the
Chapel of Eternal Love

Everyone savored the deliciously, decadent chocolate mousse along with their coffee and champagne, as they listened to the speeches and tributes rendered by Chad as host, and Mark as Rosemary's employer. Pastor Glen, frail as he was, took the microphone and paid tribute to the lady who had been so loyal to the chapel and embodied the very values he had hoped to create as a testament to his beloved wife, Laura. More than once, Rosemary wiped the tears from her eyes.

Kid Galahad, the Elvis impersonator, gently opened the door to the Celebration Room and quietly tip-toed in. He placed a large wrapped box on the gift table. As soon as the speeches were over, right on cue, he took one strum of the guitar and struck a dramatic pose. All heads turned. It was a typical Kid Galahad entrance. He burst into his crowd-pleasing "Viva Las Vegas." This was always a hit, and, with many tourists present, he knew this evening's event would be no exception. Everyone was mesmerized when "The Kid," as he was also known, maneuvered around the room working his audience. The Elvis contingent from Tennessee was enthralled, and they bobbed back and forth in their chairs, clapping their hands, and snapping their fingers.

On the other side of the dance floor, and much less

enamored, was Buster. From the sound of the first guitar strum, he sat up from his nestled position by Emmy's feet and started to howl. Emmy quickly, yet quietly, picked him up in her arms and edged along the side of the room, out into the crystal chandelier-laden hallway with its bright-red carpet. She was familiar with Kid Galahad. Their paths had crossed on several occasions.

Gee, Buster sure is deceptively heavy, she thought as she put him on the floor, stooped beside him, and stroked his forehead. "Now, you don't want to spoil things for The Kid, do you?" Buster licked her hand. "No, I didn't think so," she said. "We'll just wait here until he's finished." She led him to a nearby chair, where she sat down and watched the world go by. Buster still whimpered softly, but she managed to keep the noise subdued by rubbing his cheeks and running her fingers along his nose.

Back at the party, Kid Galahad finished his opening song and took to the center of the stage. "For all you couples in love, this song's for you," he said and segued into the slow ballad, "Love Me Tender." Mitch put his arm around Diana, and the twins followed. Julian and Hayley looked at each other and held hands. The atmosphere in the room turned quiet and romantic. The Kid had the audience eating out of his hand.

Keeping in true Elvis character and knowing the evening was not about him, he introduced his final number. "I wrote this song for my mother. Many of you will not remember it. Many of you may not have heard it. But I think it is a fitting tribute to Rosemary. I know I speak for all my impersonators in Las Vegas." The crowd laughed. He started to play "That's Someone You Never Forget" as he slowly made his way to

Rosemary's table and serenaded her. Everyone could tell it was a heartfelt rendition. Most were not familiar with the song, but Bobby, Mavis, Val, and Mike were fully aware and sang quietly along with the impersonator.

When finished, The Kid leaned over and kissed Rosemary's hand. "It's been a pleasure knowing you. Thank you for always being so gracious," he said and smiled. The applause was loud and continuous. Elvis and Cilla whistled loudly from their table.

The entertainer returned to the stage and took a bow. "I believe it is now time for dancing," he said. "Please enjoy yourselves." He gestured to the band to resume their positions, and the music started back up. Many of the couples headed to the floor and started to move to the rhythm of the music. Rosemary began to make her way around the tables and greet those whose faces she remembered, some more familiar than others, and to those who she knew had traveled distances to be there.

With Buster having resumed his quiet state, Emmy returned to the party and visited with Giovanni and Becky, whom she had not seen since they were all at the chapel five years earlier. Giovanni greeted her effusively, kissing her on both cheeks. "We never did get together, and we really must," he said excitedly. "I'll never forget you giving me your wedding bouquet of orchids," Becky said to Emmy as they hugged.

Rosemary was conversing with Congresswoman Kathleen Maxwell and her husband Kurt. "I am so sorry," she said noticing his prosthesis. Kathleen interjected, trying to avoid discussing unpleasantries on such a festive occasion. "We've never forgotten how you made our wedding day complete. You helped me with my hair, my change of clothes, even had a little bouquet for me. I was in such a state that day." Rosemary smiled at her.

Renee overheard the conversation. "She saved our wedding, too," said the former model with gratitude in her voice. "The media were like vultures. Rosemary made it so we at least had some dignity to our ceremony. We will remember it always." She searched for Peter who was still clicking his camera around the room.

"You're all too kind," said Rosemary. Her eyes fell on Mattie, and she hugged the young widow. "Father Roades told me about your loss. I'm so very sorry."

"Thank you," Mattie replied, not wishing to dwell on the subject. "I may be moving to Las Vegas. I'm meeting with Peter and Renee about a possible position with their company on Monday."

Kid Galahad walked up and stalled any further conversation. Still in his Elvis character, "Would you like to dance?" he asked Mattie. She couldn't help but like and be charmed by the fun-loving impersonator. "Sure," she said. They headed onto the dance floor.

From across the room, Cory and Heidi watched The Kid gyrate back and forth.

"He's amazing," said Heidi. "He could just as easily be the real thing. I wonder where they discovered him?"

Mavis overheard the comment from her neighboring table. "Oh, he sang at our wedding. We decided to renew our vows while we're here and asked him to come sing for us again. We told him about the event tonight, and he offered to come and sing for free."

"When are you renewing your vows?" Cory asked. "The

chapel was booked solid when we inquired."

"The very last appointment tomorrow afternoon," Bobby said in his southern drawl. "The six of us are renewing our vows. Hey, you're sure welcome to renew yours at our ceremony, as long as you're okay with Kid Galahad." It was a typical gesture of what the Tennesseans considered southern hospitality.

"Of course," Cory chuckled. "Though, we should probably check with Father Roades to see if he's agreeable to having a group ceremony."

Taylor and Sherri had been sitting at the same table as the Elvis aficionados all evening. "Count us in," said Taylor much to the chagrin of Sherri, who tugged at his hand. "What's the matter?" he whispered.

"What am I going to wear?" said an agitated Sherri.

Taylor kissed her on the cheek and patted her hand. "Whatever you choose, you'll look beautiful."

I don't deserve this man, she thought.

Bobby and Cory headed toward where Mark was seated with Pastor Glen and offered their suggestion of a group ceremony.

"Absolutely," Mark said. "The more the merrier."

"In that case, let's see who else would like to participate," said Bobby. He waited for the band to finish their number, asked for the microphone, and requested a show of hands from the assembled group who wanted to join them for a mass renewal of wedding vows.

Cory and Heidi immediately raised their hands, as did the twins—Lester with his left hand and Chester with his right. Julian and Hayley followed. By this time, Rosemary was standing behind Mitch and Diana. Mitch reached for Diana's hand. "Please," he pleaded. "Let's give it one more try. This is a sign." Diana, noticing the glass of water in front of him, was aware he hadn't drunk anything that evening. She paused for a moment, then nodded. Mitch heaved a sigh of relief, raised a hand, holding one of Diana's tightly with the other. Rosemary smiled. She did not recall why, but this was one of the couples whose marriage she was not sure would last.

Mark looked at Sarah. "We can arrange for you and your husband to be picked up for the vow renewal," he said.

"Oh, I don't think so," she replied. Oscar suddenly became agitated and started prodding the table gently with his fist. Sarah and Mark looked at him. Oscar smiled at Mark and nodded his head up and down. "I think he wants to come tomorrow," said Mark. Oscar nodded again.

Sarah thought for a moment. "Okay. If you can arrange for us to be picked up, that would be lovely." She reached for Oscar's hand.

Rosa knew her work shift would interfere, but desperately wanted to attend. By renewing her vows with Ernesto her memories of the chapel would not be so painful. She glanced in Pru's direction, searching for a signal. Pru happened to be looking at her, knowing exactly what was going through her employee's mind. She smiled and nodded to Rosa, who beamed back, clasped her hands as if in prayer, and bowed slightly, expressing her gratitude.

Linh was delighted when she saw her parents confirm their desire to be part of the ceremony. She thought back over the years spent tracking down her father after the Vietnam conflict and all the accompanying uncertainty when her mother came to live in the United States.

Rosemary saw Derek and Betty-Sue at the next table alongside Rosa and Ernesto and made her way to greet them. She remembered so well their pain and angst. They both hugged Rosemary, and Betty-Sue said "If Father Roades will permit, maybe we can bring your namesake, our little Rosemary, to the renewal ceremony tomorrow."

As if hearing her plea, and noticing all the hands raised, Mark seized the microphone from Bobby. "Any parents, aunts, uncles, cousins, brothers and sisters, not to mention children, are welcome to come. It will also be the last ceremony Rosemary will witness."

Pastor Glen could not believe his eyes and ears. He shivered as he felt the spirit of Laura alongside him.

"I wish now we had brought little Jasmine with us," said Hayley.

"Me too," said Julian. "But at least it's been a treat for Mum and Dad."

Buster tugged at his leash and started to whine. Emmy stood up and loosened her hold to see where he wanted to go. He headed straight for Mattie's table, whose eyes were cast downward. Emmy sensed something wrong and sat in the chair vacated by Peter, who was still darting around the room capturing the event on his camera. She reached out for Mattie's hand. The widow looked up, a stoic expression on her face, even though her eyes were moist with tears.

"I lost my husband," said Mattie. "Tomorrow at the chapel would be a sobering reminder of him. I don't think I can handle it."

Emmy thought for a moment, remembering her own unhappy day at the chapel. "Maybe just being there will bring some comfort. Sometimes that happens. Tomorrow will be my first day of work at the chapel. We can sit together, perhaps with Rosemary. You won't be alone."

"You may be right. I'll think about it. Thank you for being so caring."

Emmy squeezed her hand.

"Okay," yelled Kid Galahad. "Looks like there will be a full house at the chapel tomorrow afternoon. Now everybody, let's get back to the party. What happened to the music?" He started to clap his hands in the air and headed to the dance floor where he began to move and groove by himself.

Emmy returned to her table.

The band commenced playing again, as Bobby and Mavis, Val and Mike, and Elvis and Cilla took to the floor. They were soon joined by Sherri and Taylor. It was not long before the floor was filled with everyone dancing the night away. Pru finally felt relaxed enough over the evening's event to have a dance with Chad. She was so proud of him.

Sarah looked at her watch, and suggested to Mark that maybe it was time to return Oscar to the home.

"Sure thing. Do you mind running them home, Emmy?"

"Of course not," Emmy responded.

"I hate to take you away from such a lovely evening," Sarah said.

"Not at all. I have a long day tomorrow. It's the first day at my new job." She laughed.

"Looks like we'll see you tomorrow," Sarah said to Rosemary. "Please extend our gratitude to the hosts. I hate to interrupt them while they're dancing. They look so happy together."

Mark started to wheel Oscar's chair toward the door. Sarah held onto Emmy's arm while Emmy kept Buster on a tight leash with her other hand.

Rosemary bent down. "Now, you be a good boy, won't you?" she said to Buster, stroking his brow, and fighting back the tears. Buster started licking her cheek. It was as if he understood. She stood back up.

Emmy said nothing, but hugged Rosemary. Sarah and Emmy followed Mark to the door as Emmy quickly stopped by the gift table to pick up the basket of goodies for Buster.

Rosemary watched Buster waddle out the door, then she sat down, tears streaming down her face. She knew saying goodbye, the next day, to her sweet Buster would be one of the hardest things she'd ever have to do. Pastor Glen put his arms around her, hoping to provide some comfort. He looked forward to seeing everyone the next day, when they would all return to the Chapel of Eternal Love.

Chapter 22

Gifts of Love

The evening was starting to wind down, and one by one the guests began to leave. Everyone was in high spirits; all looked forward to reuniting at the chapel the next day.

Derek and Betty-Sue were among the last to leave and stopped by the main table to say their farewells. "It was so nice of you to invite all the families tomorrow, Father Mark. Derek's parents are here, so I'm sure they'll come. Sadly, mine won't," she said. Rosemary recalled the turmoil of the couple's wedding day, and gave her a look of understanding.

Julian and Hayley thanked Pru and Chad for hosting and offered to make little bridal bouquets out of the centerpieces for all the ladies attending the renewal ceremony the next day. "If you keep them somewhere safe and cool, we'll be happy to re-arrange the orchids. They should keep their freshness for quite a while," said Hayley.

"What a wonderful idea and a charming gesture," remarked Pru. "That will be lovely and greatly appreciated by all the ladies, I'm sure. They really *are* the most beautiful orchids."

Julian grinned at the guest of honor. "We do hope you like the orchids in your room, Rosemary. They're also from our plantation in Hawaii." Rosemary looked confused.

"Now, you've spoiled the surprise," said Chad.

Pru laughed. "We're not taking you home tonight. You're

spending the night as our guest. Come on, let's go upstairs," she said reaching for Rosemary's arm.

Rosemary was stunned. "But I've nothing to wear. I have no overnight bag or anything."

"Everything is taken care of. Go ahead and take her up, my sweet," said Chad. "I'll arrange for some of the staff to bring all the gifts to her room."

"I'm so sorry for messing things up," Julian said. "I wasn't aware it was a surprise."

"Not a problem," replied Chad. "Everything went smoothly tonight, so no big deal." He patted Julian on the shoulder.

Pru and Rosemary stepped into the elevator, their arms linked. Rosemary was in for another surprise when they exited and stood in front of the door marked *Penthouse Suite*. Pru unlocked the door, and Rosemary entered the room with its spectacular view of the neon signs illuminated up and down the strip. In the background, the residential lights in the other parts of Las Vegas were twinkling and shimmering, creating a magnificent backdrop.

As she admired the vista in front of her, Rosemary was speechless. Slowly, she looked around the living room at the silk covered furniture and decorative accents with touches of gold. Pru took her by the arm and escorted her through the rest of the spacious and elegantly decorated rooms.

"I'll be lost in this gigantic bed," said Rosemary, walking into the bedroom and noticing the nightgown laid out for her. "And I could certainly drown in that colossal bath tub," she said as she looked into the marble bathroom.

Chad was heard directing the staff in the next room. "Just put the gifts on the table here."

After the staff left, the two ladies joined him. "Anyone for a nightcap?" he asked, holding a bottle of champagne in his hand and popping the cork.

"One for the road," laughed Pru.

The three of them sat for a while and relived the party, talking of all the people who had attended, as they sipped bubbly from the crystal flutes.

"It has to be the most memorable evening of my life, even though I had to part with my Buster." Rosemary sniffed and pulled a handkerchief from her purse. "But I know he's going to a good home."

Pru and Chad finished their champagne and rose to leave. "You must be tired," she said to Rosemary.

"Tired, but happy. So very happy," replied Rosemary. They all hugged. "How can I ever thank you?"

"Just sleep well and enjoy the suite," said Pru. They said goodnight and left.

Rosemary turned and stared out the window again. Actually, she was not tired at all and was way too excited to sleep. She surveyed the room once more and saw the arrangement of orchids that Julian had spoken of earlier. The little note card alongside read, "*A bouquet of good wishes for your future happiness. Thank you for playing the piano at our wedding, and for being a special part of our happiness that day.*"

She saw the mass of gifts on the large, glass coffee table and decided to open them.

The first one was no surprise. It was a lovely gift basket wrapped in cellophane displaying an assortment of *Repent* products. Through the transparent paper, she saw a small bottle of eau de cologne, containers of face and hand cream, some bath salts, and a round canister of talcum powder neatly placed beneath the monogrammed powder puff. *Maybe the R does signify Repent,* she thought. *But, I'll just pretend it's for Rosemary,* and chuckled at her own little joke. She removed the note from the envelope. *"You made our wedding day magical and memorable,"* it said. *"May your many memories at the chapel be equally as magical.—Renee & Peter."*

Rosemary smiled when she removed paper from the next gift and revealed a large framed picture of Elvis. He was sporting his trademark rhinestone-studded trousers, guitar in one hand, the other outstretched in the air. The photo was signed by all the impersonators in Las Vegas. The card simply read, *"From all of us—The Kid."*

I suspect this is also a picture, thought Rosemary, picking up the next gift and unwrapping it. Instead, she found a framed proclamation from the Congress of the United States House of Representatives in recognition of her dedicated service to all the residents of her congressional district. *Who in the world gave me this?* She read the message from Congresswoman Maxwell and realized what should have been obvious. *"Thought this was most appropriate so I arranged with your House Representative who is a good friend of mine. Hope you like it. It is well deserved—Kathleen and Kurt."*

I can't imagine what's in this one. Rosemary lifted the surprisingly light, yet bulky package. The card attached was from Mattie. *"My wedding day at the chapel was the happiest day of my life. Hoping that your retirement will be as happy, and that this will keep you warm throughout those cold winters—Mattie."* The present was a Harley-Davidson women's fleece jacket. Rosemary tried it on for size and was surprised at how comfortable it was. She made her way to the bedroom and looked at herself in the mirror. *I'm probably too old to be wearing something like this, but it will be handy if I need to run down to the store. It was sweet of Mattie to think of me.* She removed the jacket and returned to the living room, and picked up the next gift.

Such beautiful wrapping paper. It's almost a shame to open it. But she did anyway. *How nice. A beautiful souvenir book of Las Vegas.* Rosemary turned the page and read the inscription. *"Hope you will never forget the marriage capital of the world."* It was signed, *Lester, Chester, Molly, Dolly, and Children* with Lester's signature on the left and Chester's on the right. Dolly and Molly's names were penned almost identically between both husbands. One of them had artistically drawn four little happy faces.

Rosemary read the card on another gift. *"Gracias. I remember your kindness to me always. I make this myself with wool from my native country. I hope you like it. My world here with my husband is no possible without your help—Rosa y Ernesto"* It was a beautiful multi-colored scarf which she wrapped around her neck. *How sweet and how thoughtful.*

She was unaware that Cory and Heidi arrived at the very last minute, not knowing of the party or their need for a gift. Nonetheless, they were able to find in one of the hotel stores a pretty souvenir charm bracelet of Las Vegas. Rosemary liked the *"Congratulations on your Retirement"* card, with the message *"May the best of times be yet to come—Cory, Heidi & Courtney."*

Rosemary took a break. *Since this is such a special evening, I think I'll have more bubbly.* She poured herself another glass, even though she was not accustomed to drinking, but this occasion called for it. She lay on the couch for a minute with her feet up and absorbed the generosity of all the kind and lovely people. Buster went through her mind, and she wondered how he was settling in with Emmy, and then concerned herself as to how Emmy was coping with the loveable pooch. *Well, tomorrow will come soon enough, and I'll find out.* She looked at her watch. It was just past midnight. *Bewitching hour.* She sat up and returned to opening the seemingly never-ending assortment of boxes and packages.

There were two small presents, and she opened them one after the other. Both were brooches. One was from Emmy. The brooch held colorful rhinestones in the shape of a heart held by an alloy frame. "*Always keep your heart filled with love—Emmy*" read the card. The other brooch was from Sherri and Taylor—two hearts made out of Cubic Zirconia. "*From our hearts to yours—Sherri & Taylor.*"

Rosemary had always sensed both Emmy and Sherri may have had colorful pasts, and now considered it strange they should both have given her gifts with hearts. *I suspect these are from their personal jewelry collection. How very endearing. They are giving something of themselves.*

A long envelope contained a gift certificate for a massage at a beauty salon in Carson City. "*My friend there will take good care of you—Diana and Mitch.*"

"Now, that will certainly come in handy. Once I have moved, I'll need that," said Rosemary to no one, imagining herself being pampered. "Wonder what is in this gift bag?" She removed the tissue paper and lifted an oblong, wooden box with a picture of Elvis painted on it. Raising the lid revealed a red velvet-lined jewelry box. The tune "Love Me" started to play. Rosemary remembered the song from when Elvis sang it on the Ed Sullivan Show many years earlier. *Where have the years gone?* She listened as the song played over and over. Eventually, she closed the lid and the music stopped. *As if I can't guess who this is from.* Sure enough, the card read "*From the gang at Elvis Memorabilia. Now ya'll come out and visit us, ya hear.*" Rosemary picked up the two brooches and placed them in the jewelry box.

There were four gifts left. There was another photograph—a portrait of Derek and Betty-Sue holding little Rosemary and was signed, "*With love and gratitude—Derek, Betty-Sue and your namesake.*" Rosemary clutched the photo close as all the memories of that day, and many other days came flooding back. Her eyes welled up again. *Oh stop it, you old fool,* she chided herself, dabbing her eyes with her handkerchief.

This looks like another piece of jewelry. Rosemary opened the little cloth sack containing a Kabbalah 72 name pendant. Rosemary had witnessed and heard rituals and customs from all faiths and beliefs while at the chapel. She was fully versed with the tenets of Kabbalah and knew the significance of the wheeled necklace. She recalled one of the wedding couples mentioning how the amulet was meant for anyone and was intended to enhance positive changes in people's lives. *I hope that's true for me. I sure will be going through lots of changes. What a charming and considerate gift.*

She removed the card from the next box and opened it. "*Love and happiness, always—Oscar and Sarah.*" The accompanying box contained three lace handkerchiefs embroidered ornately with the word "love". *Bless their hearts. Life must be so hard for them both.* Rosemary shook her head in amazement.

Now, holding the final package, she noticed the congratulatory message was from Phil and Kim-Ly, recognizing her friend Phil's handwriting. *"Kim made this for you. It was a hobby of hers when she lived in Vietnam. It is a much practiced art there. We hope you will like it and find a place for it in your new home."* The gift was a sand painting arranged in the image of the Chapel of Eternal Love. Rosemary knew the adoration and pride Phil had for his wife. *This is just beautiful. Simply beautiful.* She sat for a moment admiring the artistry and love that had gone into making the gift.

Overwhelmed by the generosity of everyone, she was still in a state of shock that so many people would attend such an extravagant party in her honor, much less bring gifts. Pinching her arm to see if everything was real or whether she was in a dream world, she wandered through the rooms again, absorbing the beauty and plush surroundings, yet missing the pitter-patter of Buster's little paws.

It was now past one o'clock in the morning, and knowing the next day would be an emotional roller coaster for her, she was still too overcome with emotion to go to bed. She spotted the mahogany desk in the corner and switched on the lamp. Upon opening the drawer, she observed a pile of neatly stacked notepaper with the Bella Del Mundo name and logo alongside a pack of matching envelopes. Sitting in the comfortable swivel chair, she removed the stationery, picked up the monogrammed pen, and started to write her thank you notes.

Chapter 23

Farewell Rosemary

Everyone was gathering outside the chapel. It was late afternoon, and the sun was trying to peek through the clouds. It had rained for most of the day, and a beautiful rainbow now provided a breathtaking backdrop to the chapel. Rosemary was inside, behind the altar, rearranging a large vase of red roses when Rosa and Ernesto walked in with their four young boys, and approached her.

"Señora Rosemary, I want you meet my husband. I no have chance last night at party to speak with you."

Rosemary turned from the flowers and hugged Rosa.

"I no have operation on my eyes if not for you," said Ernesto. "I thank you from heart always."

Rosemary shook her head. "No, it is Mr. and Mrs. Nelson, who you need to thank—and your lovely wife. She has worked very hard." She smiled at them. "And look at these handsome young men." The boys beamed.

Betty-Sue and Derek entered the chapel. "We thought you'd like to meet your namesake," said Derek. His wife handed the baby to Rosemary to hold.

"She's beautiful," said Rosemary, kissing the baby's cheek. "I'm so proud and happy for you both."

Outside, Buster was mingling throughout the crowd, licking legs, sniffing shoes, and occasionally trying to jump up at some of the attendees, but most times his paws missed the intended target. Buster desperately tried to dodge Elvis and Cilla's five-year-old twin girls, much to the dismay of the parents, whose pleas to leave the dog alone fell on deaf ears.

Dolly and Molly held their babies as their husbands stood proudly behind them, exchanging baby experiences with Mattie, since their children were all the same age. Mattie, holding baby Garth, was wondering whether attending this ceremony was such a good idea, after all. She stooped down to pat Buster and show the dog to her son.

Emmy was passing out the rearranged bouquets of orchids, uniquely designed by Julian and Hayley. "I'm not sure I qualify for one," said Mattie.

"Of course you do," Emmy said, gently placing a bouquet into Mattie's hands. "In your heart and soul, I'm sure you'll still renew your vows."

They were joined by Taylor and Sherri, who introduced themselves to Emmy.

"Ah yes," Emmy stated. "You're the couple who left the basket of treats for Buster. That little dog stayed with me last night, and I can assure you he enjoyed many of those doggie goodies. I've kept the wrappers, so I know which ones to get in the future, especially since Buster will be living with me from now on."

"Let me know if we can help," said Taylor giving her his card. Sherri and I are both dog lovers. I help out at the animal shelter." Buster was nuzzling his feet.

Peter was circulating through the crowd getting the attendees to sign their names in the souvenir photo album he had hastily compiled to present to Rosemary.

"Mommy, there's that same lady we saw last time we were here. The one who's wearing so much lipstick." Courtney pointed to Sherri.

"Hush!" said Heidi, admonishing her daughter. "It's rude to point."

A cream-colored Volvo pulled into the parking lot, and two couples emerged. Becky shook her head in disbelief. "Oh no! Leave it to my mother. Not only was she absent on my wedding day, but now, here she is dressed in black on the day I'm renewing my vows."

"Well, at least they're here," said Giovanni. "Not only that, our folks even carpooled. I suppose we've made some progress. Maybe, they'll all feel happier when we share our news."

Esther stood at the side of the car staring at the chapel. "Well, it's not quite the ceremony at the synagogue we planned for our daughter, is it Jacob?"

"Nor the cathedral I had in mind for our Giovanni." Mario nudged his wife, Gina, for confirmation.

Becky and Giovanni greeted their parents with hugs. "Before we go in, we have some wonderful news we want to share with you," said Becky, ignoring her mother's choice of apparel. "You're going to be grandparents this summer. We hope this makes you happy."

Esther opened her arms and embraced her daughter. "Finally! We thought we would go to our graves never knowing our grandchildren. I'm sure Mario and Gina felt the same."

Gina gave her son a big hug, too. "We're so excited for you. Maybe we can all help pick out baby names. Yes?"

"Too late for that. We've already decided. Persimmon if it's a girl, Declan if it's a boy," announced Becky.

Esther was incredulous. She glared at her daughter, repeating the name slowly and deliberately.

"Persimmon? You'd call your daughter Persimmon? What's wrong with a nice, traditional name like Hannah or Ruth?"

"I also think it would be nice if you chose to name your son after your old man, Giovanni," said Mario.

"Why? You didn't name me after your old man, Pop," Giovanni replied.

"But Persimmon?" Esther continued. "What level-headed person would call their daughter Persimmon?"

Thank goodness, Emmy is going to save the day, thought Becky as she saw Emmy walking toward them with the bouquets.

Chad and Pru pulled into the parking lot. Chad helped Oscar into his wheelchair, while Pru helped Pastor Glen out of the back seat. Sarah straightened her husband's tie and followed Chad as he pushed the wheelchair toward the solid-oak front door. Pru took Sarah's arm as Emmy approached them with the bouquets, which they accepted gratefully.

"Let me help you, Pastor Glen," Emmy said, assisting the frail minister to his seat inside the chapel.

"Time to go in, everyone. We'll be starting shortly," said Mark from the chapel entrance.

"Thank you so much for coming," said Betty-Sue to her in-laws. She linked her arm into Derek's, who was carrying little Rosemary, as they turned to head through the chapel door.

The sound of a car screeching as it swerved into the parking lot caused everyone's heads to turn. Betty-Sue couldn't believe her eyes. "Daddy," she yelled and ran down the steps into the parking lot to greet both parents who were exiting the beige sedan.

"Princess," said Ed. "Can you ever forgive your father for being such a stubborn old fool all these years?" He hugged and kissed his daughter on the head, as Sally, his wife, looked on joyfully. *Finally, a reunion! It's a miracle,* she thought.

"How did you even know we were renewing our vows today?" asked Betty-Sue.

"I guess Rosemary found our phone number from her records and called us this morning. She's something else. Then, shortly afterwards, Derek's folks called and said they'd be here."

"Thanks for coming, sir," said Derek, who had followed his wife. He shook hands with his father-in-law and kissed his mother-in-law on the cheek. "Nice to see you again, Sally."

"Let me hold my granddaughter," said Ed, as he reached out his arms. Derek handed him the baby.

"We need to go in," said Betty-Sue. "The ceremony will begin pretty soon."

Everyone headed into the chapel. All the couples, soon to renew their vows, were seated at the front. Parents and other family members occupied the rear pews, along with Kid Galahad. Linh also decided to sit in the back instead of next to her parents, Phil and Kim-Ly. *This is their day. I'll just be an observer.*

Emmy was just about to sit down by Rosemary who was in the last row, when she saw Mattie, carrying baby Garth, walk in. She could tell Mattie seemed uncertain as to what to do, or where to go.

Mattie caught her breath on seeing the inside of chapel for

the first time since her wedding. Memories of that day came flooding back. *Emmy is right. I do feel a sense of happiness being here.*

In a way, Emmy identified with what Mattie must be feeling, since Emmy, too, was there without a husband. She reached into her purse, removed a card and went to Mattie, handing it to her. "If you do decide to move to Las Vegas, you're welcome to stay with me and Buster while you're looking for a job or a place to live."

"Wow! That's *so* nice of you. You never know, I may just need to take you up on that. I can't get over how kind everyone is."

"That's because we're not really sin city. We're a city of love," Emmy replied.

About that time, Renee turned around in her seat, saw Mattie, and patted the empty space alongside her.

"Go on," said Emmy. "I think you might feel better being part of the ceremony, not just observing it." Mattie gave Emmy a hug and moved to sit with Renee and Peter.

A good-looking gentleman walked in from the side of the chapel and went to the front. Hayley immediately recognized the gondolier from the Venetian Hotel who had sung at their wedding.

"Julian," she whispered excitedly. "Look who it is."

"I know," he grinned. "I tracked him down this morning once I knew we were going to have this ceremony."

"But it's not *our* ceremony. We're really guests of the Elvis folks from Tennessee."

"Don't worry," he whispered back. "I already spoke to them. They're good with it, as is Father Roades."

Rosemary leaned over and spoke softly to Emmy. "Can you play the piano?"

"Of course. If I know the song he is going to sing, I'll be happy to play," she responded, heading to the piano.

"This song is for all of you today. May it always be so," said the gondolier. He started to sing in his strong, baritone voice, *"I give to you, and you give to me, true love, true love."* Emmy recognized the song and his key and began playing, humming the song softly and wistfully.

When they finished, the gondolier sat in the back row alongside The Kid, as Emmy returned to be with Rosemary. Buster nestled contently at their feet.

Mark made his way to the altar and started to speak. He was pleased to see Mitch and Diana in the front row and smiled at them. Seeing Pastor Glen sitting alongside them at the end of the row, Mark couldn't believe how thoughtless he had been.

"Excuse me, ladies and gentlemen. I had planned exactly what I was going to say to you today, but far better, we have with us, Pastor Glen, who built this very chapel. Pastor Glen, could I impose on you to do the honors at this very special ceremony?"

The elderly minister was taken aback, but realized that now he was retired this might be the last ceremony he would ever be called upon to perform. *What a truly fitting tribute to my beloved Laura,* he mused.

"Why ... I'd be the one who is honored," he said, as he rose from his seat, and with the help of his cane, walked slowly toward the altar. As he arrived, he caught the sweet scent of the flowers nearby and spent a few seconds admiring the large vase of red roses. *How nice they were able to find Laura's favorite flowers this time of year.* He looked out at the mosaic glass windows and at all the assembled faces in front of him, sensing the love and joy all around. Recognizing the changing of the guard from Rosemary to Emmy, and noting their attentive looks, he knew the baton was being passed from one kind and loving soul to another. Indeed, Laura's life had not been in vain. He silently gave thanks to his creator and started his service.

After the ceremony was completed, there were more than a few tear-filled eyes. Emmy was busy dabbing her face with her handkerchief. Sherri and Sarah were both drying their moist eyes.

"My dear," said Rosemary, as she held Emmy's other hand. "You will be part of the love and joy of all couples who come through these doors. Believe me, it will provide you not only happiness but comfort, when needed. It will be a true sanctuary for you."

"I do hope you will come back and visit," smiled Emmy, still drying her eyes.

"Let's promise to keep in touch regularly, at the very least," Rosemary replied.

Mark joined his fellow minister and requested Rosemary join them. She rose from her seat and headed to the altar. Not one to take credit, Mark presented the photo album to her. "Rosemary, may this compilation of chapel photos and the signed pictures of the attendees here today, provide you with many wonderful memories as you start your new life. It has been put together for you by our photographer extraordinaire, Peter Sharpstone." He gestured to where Peter and Renee were sitting. Everyone applauded as Rosemary, once again, was left speechless.

"I can't think of anything sensible to say," she stammered. "Other than, whatever small part in your happiness I may have played has been given back to me by all who have passed through these doors over the years. Especially, all of you who came back for the party last night and who are here today." She fought back the tears as Buster trotted to the altar and sat beside her. Wishing to deflect the attention from herself, she hastily added, "I believe there has been a request for Kid Galahad to sing for us."

Always ready to perform, The Kid leaped to his feet and starting singing "Won't you wear my ring, around your neck?" Buster lifted his head and started to howl at the top of his doggie lungs, as Rosemary left the altar and returned to the back of the chapel. It was Emmy's turn to put her arm around Rosemary and offer comfort. Buster continued his serenade along with The Kid, so they gathered him up and crept outside. It was a little cold and almost dark. The Kid finished his song, and Mark could be heard talking to the crowd, although neither Emmy nor Rosemary could decipher exactly what was being said. Couple by couple, the chapel began to empty out.

"There you are, Rosemary," said Phil. "Kim and I were wondering where you were. Are you ready? Dinner is waiting. Boy, Kim has outdone herself and made something really special tonight. Mark will be joining us as soon as everything is locked up."

"You go. I'll stay and help Mark," said Emmy, hugging Rosemary. "I need to learn how to close the chapel at the end of each day."

Rosemary stooped down and played with Buster one last time. She rubbed his ears and gave him a final rub under his chin. A lump in her throat precluded her from saying anything.

Kim-Ly put her arm around her dinner guest and steered her toward the car. There were shouts of "Goodbye Rosemary" and "Good Luck" from the group on the steps. Phil opened the door, and Rosemary turned to look at the chapel for a final time. Tightly clutched under her arm was the photo album. Buster made one last dash toward her, barking as he went, but stopped short at the car door. Rosemary leaned over and gave him a tearful kiss before getting in the car. Phil started the engine and slowly pulled out of the driveway.

Buster, his eyes forlorn, wagged his tail slowly, as he watched the automobile drive off into the distance. Rosemary waved at him through the rear window until he and the chapel disappeared from her sight.

About the Author

Stephen Murray is the author of "The Chapel of Eternal Love." This is his second published novel. He has also completed a murder mystery scheduled for publication. Stephen was born in England and raised in different countries throughout Southern Africa. Upon completion of his high school education, he returned to England before moving to California in 1976. Stephen has travelled extensively throughout the world. He owns a computer software company. Apart from travelling and writing, he enjoys all the arts and current affairs. Stephen makes his home in Las Vegas, Nevada, where he has lived since May 2003.

For questions, comments, or to order additional copies of this book, please visit **www.thechapelofeternallove.com**, email him at stephen@casandras.net, or write to:

Casandras
9811 W. Charleston Blvd., Ste. 2-354
Las Vegas, NV 89117

4/22

CPSIA information can be obtained
at www.ICGtesting.com
Printed in the USA
LVHW042349040919
630007LV00009B/191/P

9 780991 194018